Kitty Valentine
dates a Fireman

Spin the wheel.
date the guy.
jillian dodd

Kitty Valentine dates a Fireman

JILLIAN DODD

Jillian Dodd, Inc.
Madeira Beach, FL
Jillian Dodd is a registered trademark of Jillian Dodd, Inc.
Kitty Valentine™ is a trademark of Jillian Dodd, Inc.

Editor: Jovana Shirley, Unforeseen Editing,
www.unforeseenediting.com

ISBN: 978-1-946793-99-7

Books by Jillian Dodd

Chapter One

FUN FACT ABOUT me, Kitty Valentine, best-selling romance author: I have a surprisingly high tolerance for pain.

Not emotional pain, mind you. Just the opposite. I'm what my best friend, Hayley, would refer to as a drama queen. The first time she called me that, I had to pick myself up off the floor where I'd just thrown myself to tell her how wrong she was.

Physical pain, on the other hand, I can handle. Probably a side effect of being rather clumsy and prone to accidents. If there's a one-in-a-hundred shot of somebody falling into a mall fountain while texting, I'm the one dripping wet with a broken phone.

Yet there is no pain, either physical or emotional, that can compete with lunch at Grandmother's. Oh, the cringing. The slow, silent inner death as she questions each and every one of my life choices while managing to embarrass me with tales of her own flawed choices.

The best part? I brought Hayley with me this time to give my grandmother somebody else's life to dissect, and what is she doing? Is she taking the heat off me the way a decent best friend should? Is she steering the conversation toward positive aspects of my life? Good decisions I've made lately?

Is she using the prepared list of talking points that I slaved over for hours in advance of this lunch date?

"I think she should cut her hair. What do you think?" Hayley gestures to me with her knife, which she might as well slide into my back while she's at it.

Grandmother, whose hair is always gleaming and perfect, studies me with her sharp blue eyes. "Hmm. I do prefer Kathryn with long hair, but I see what you mean."

It takes all the self-control in my body to keep my hands away from the brown waves tumbling over my shoulders. *What the heck is wrong with my hair?*

"Not *short*, short, mind you." Hayley tilts her head to the side. "But shoulder-length. She looks so cute with shorter hair."

"I can't disagree."

"Do I get a say in this?" I whisper, looking back and forth between them. "Because I can leave the room if you're gonna keep talking about me like I'm not here."

"Don't say *gonna*." My grandmother sniffs the air like she smells something foul. "It's low-class."

"You should hear some of the things that come

out of Hayley's mouth if you think that's low-class."

Hayley gets a big smile from me after that.

"What Hayley says is her business."

"Why isn't what I say my business?"

"And she needs to refresh her wardrobe," Hayley adds before popping an olive into her treacherous mouth. "I mean, how's she going to impress her next boyfriend, wearing last season's collections?"

"I'm going to kill you. I hope you know that." I drag a thumb across my throat for effect, which doesn't seem to make much of a difference. If anything, she smiles wider than before.

No wonder she was okay with coming to lunch today. She even seemed to look forward to it.

Because she hates me. I mean, that's literally the only explanation I can come up with. I must have done something to her long ago, and she's been planning my demise ever since. Gotta give her credit. She's done a good job of pretending to be my friend all this time.

The very mention of the B-word is basically Grandmother's trigger. "Speaking of which, have you found another boyfriend for your next writing project?"

No matter how many times I explain it, it doesn't seem to stick. Either that or she'd rather not remember things correctly. Now that I think about it, yeah, that's what she's doing. Much like the way she refuses to call me Kitty, the woman tends to believe what she wants and then basically sticks her fingers in her ears and yells to drown out everything else.

"Whoever he is, he won't be my boyfriend. He'll be the man I'm seeing and learning about, so I can write the hero of my next book."

She waves a hand. I'm surprised she can lift it, considering she's wearing her eight-carat diamond today. I have to give her points for style—when a new guest comes by, she likes to break out the big guns. "You children of today, with your special relationship words and technicalities. Not so much has changed since my day."

I know better than to make a snarky comment about that one, no matter how good it would feel in the moment to ask whether they had color TV back in her day. Besides, I know the answer.

Hayley brought charm to spare today. She leans in like she and Grandmother have a secret. "Don't pretend you don't get your share even now. Look at you. Flawless."

Grandmother laughs softly. "Oh, you should talk." I swear, I should've stayed home. "With your chic little suit. Don't tell me. Chanel."

"I know that's your favorite," Hayley purrs.

I also know she found it at a thrift store—great score, don't get me wrong, but come on. It's like they're getting married or something.

All right, I'm feeling a little mopey.

"Anyway …" I have to wait for them to quit

fawning over each other before continuing, "We haven't come up with the latest trope yet, but I have to choose one soon. Maggie wants the next book by the holidays, so they can release it in the new year."

"And her agent wants to negotiate a new contract in the new year too."

That's more like it. I knew I brought Hayley for a reason.

"That's wonderful! So, this new writing style has translated into higher sales then?" Grandmother raises her martini to me with a genuine, warm smile.

"It looks that way. Maggie's happy, which means the publisher's happy. Which means I'm happy."

Her eyes narrow ever so slightly. "Are you sure about that?"

Darn her. She's so grandmotherly when she feels like it.

"Why wouldn't I be?" My smile's a little tight. I have to consciously loosen it. "No, really, I'm thrilled. I am. Life is good. And I could easily write ten books based on what I've seen and done so far."

When Hayley chokes a little on her salad, I realize what I just said.

"I mean, you know, going places. Not. Like. Doing it. Not sex things." Yeah, that cleared things up. I'm not blushing harder than ever or anything like that.

Grandmother, meanwhile, doesn't care one way

or another. "If anything, I'd rather see you getting something more than a royalty check out of this. A good lay has a way of smoothing out any rough spots."

Which is when Hayley starts full-on choking, to the point where I'm pretty sure she'll need the Heimlich maneuver.

"No, no, I'm fine," she manages, red-faced and watery-eyed. "Just went down the wrong pipe."

"Did I say something wrong?" Grandmother is all innocence, though I know better than to believe her. "I thought I was speaking the truth. You strike me as two modern, forward-thinking young women."

Hayley jerks a thumb in my direction after sipping water to clear her throat. "We are. Well, I am. I'm not so sure about this one."

"Hush. I'm modern and forward-thinking."

"In theory, if not in practice." Hayley grins.

"Uh, I didn't think there was anything wrong with that."

"And there isn't." Grandmother laughs indulgently. "In fact, I commend Kathryn's good sense. It's one thing to know something is possible. It's another to know whether it's a good idea for oneself. Self-awareness is a commendable quality."

"Thank you."

And Hayley gets a smug look from me.

Except my grandmother isn't finished. "On the other hand …"

"I should've known," I mutter.

"There's something to be said for expanding one's horizon. Stretching yourself. Seeing what you're capable of. So many of our so-called limitations are self-imposed. We are all capable of far more than we give ourselves credit for."

Hayley rests her chin in her palm, watching and listening and soaking up every word. I'm pretty sure she's decided to be my grandmother when she grows up. Awkward since I made that decision for myself a long time ago. We'll walk around in our seventies, looking like clones of each other in Chanel and diamonds.

We could do a lot worse. I'm almost, sort of looking forward to it.

"That's why I'm stretching out of my comfort zone for these projects. I know I was wrong to throw such a hissy fit at first."

Hayley snorts. "You? Throw a hissy fit? The hell you say."

"Shut up. Anyway, I'm glad things are working out. I hated it at the time, but look, I'm still alive. It hasn't killed me." *Yet.* Hasn't killed me yet.

Here's the thing: I'm a girl who, until roughly eight months ago when my editor ordered me to start dating around or else lose my career, hadn't dated anyone since college, except for a few one-offs, which went miserably. I'm just no good at casual dating. I always end up liking a guy too much, too soon, and feeling like the world's biggest moron in the end.

Except for my last dating disaster, which was doomed to fail from the beginning. Granted, I knew there was no future for us when I went into it.

Okay, okay, I knew it but didn't want it to be true. I mean, who in their right mind wouldn't want, just a little, to end up married and neck deep in babies alongside their adolescent crush? Who just happened to, at one time, be an international superstar? Talk about living the dream.

But that's the thing about dreams. They very rarely pan out once it's time to wake up. My hurt feelings after the Dustin situation didn't stem from falling in love and having my heart broken, but from knowing he was pretty much telling me what I wanted to hear just to get me into bed—and his name into my book.

Neither of which happened. Too bad.

I don't think I'm cut out for casual dating. I really don't think so. Call me a serial monogamist or an optimist or a dork who can't hang in modern times. Whatever. It's how I'm built.

But work must be done, which to my agent means dating must be done. Which means I must keep stretching beyond my comfort zone. If I'm not careful, I'm going to owe the dentist a lot of money after gritting my teeth so much.

"Speaking of which …" Hayley reaches for her purse, where I know she has the spinner all ready and waiting.

There's a reason she keeps it rather than letting me have it. She knows I'll conveniently lose it.

"Oh, you're going to choose now?" I'm surprised Grandmother doesn't clap with excitement. "I get to witness this? How thrilling."

"Why don't you give it a spin for good luck?" I suggest. It can't hurt.

"Me?" Her eyes are perfectly round, one hand to her chest.

You'd think I asked her to perform open-heart surgery.

"Sure, go ahead." Hayley hands it to her with a look at me. "Now, you can't blame her if she lands on Santa."

Again with this. The girl won't be satisfied until I'm bouncing in Santa's lap. "I think this book would be released a little late for sexy Santa to be a worthwhile trope. Sorry about that."

We watch and wait while the list of potential tropes scrolls past on the little screen. Single daddy, bad boy, firefighter, lawyer, police, construction worker, motorcycle club, athlete … it's dizzying.

"Ooh!" Hayley squeals a little once my current trope is revealed. "A firefighter! Hot damn!"

"Firefighter, huh?" Okay. I can get behind the sexiness.

There's something painfully masculine and rugged and generally hot about a firefighter. Which, duh, is why they're such a popular character for romance writers to base their heroes on.

It's Grandmother's reaction that really and truly gives me pause. She looks downright thrilled—like the woman is about to lick her chops.

"What are you so excited about?" I laugh. "I'm the one who has to find him and date him and write a book about him."

"I just so happen to know where you can find an entire roomful of likely firefighters to choose from."

"Oh, good, because I wasn't keen on the idea of setting a fire in my apartment and hoping somebody hot responded."

She shakes her head. "Always with the quips."

"What do you have in mind?" Hayley asks.

"You girls might not know it, but I'm heavily involved in several of the city's charitable foundations. Including an endeavor to raise money for local animal shelters. I've always had a soft spot for animals, especially at this time of year when it gets so cold."

"What's that got to do with firefighters?"

"Patience," she sighs with a roll of her eyes. "As I was about to say, several of the local ladder and engine companies have agreed to offer their eligible members in a bachelor auction this weekend." She slaps the tabletop with her palms, triumphant.

"A bachelor auction?" Hayley and I say in unison as we exchange a look, eyebrows raised.

"With a banquet and such, yes." Grandmother nods. "It's perfect. You can join me as my guest and choose from any of the men who catch your eye."

"Will there be a lot of people there?" I mean, this does sound perfect, but there's one little hitch in the plan, which I don't think she's considered yet.

And why would she? She hasn't had to think about money in a long, long time. Like, her entire life.

And while I know I'm lucky to live the way I do, I'm not swanning around my Park Avenue brownstone, wearing an eight-carat diamond ring. Among other pieces of jewelry.

"Oh, yes, we sold out within a few days of announcing the event. It'll be held at The St. Regis, in the ballroom. You'll be a vision." She sits back, tipping her head from one side to the other. "We'll have to go shopping."

"Hang on." I cast a pleading look to Hayley, but she doesn't seem to understand what I'm nervous about. "How much money are we talking about? I mean, in the auction. Have you ever done anything like this before?"

"Many times." Grandmother waves a hand and nearly blinds me with her ring.

"What do bachelors normally go for by the time the bidding's done?"

She shrugs. "I think a few thousand each."

"Thousand?" Another look to Hayley, who's finally caught up with me.

"That's a little much," she murmurs with a sigh.

"Oh, did you think I would call upon you to pony up?" Grandmother's laughter trills out as she rings the bell for Peter to come and clear away our plates. "Please. Obviously, I'll write the check."

"I can't ask you to do that."

"You aren't asking. I'm telling you, Kathryn. You have no idea what a thrill this will be for me, watching you pick your next boyfriend."

"Not my boyfriend." I look to Peter for help when he comes in. "She's going to buy me a date at an auction, Peter. What am I supposed to do?"

He smiles as he picks up the plates. "Thank her and be done with it. You know as well as I do how pointless it is to argue with her."

The man is absolutely correct.

Chapter Two

I'M HALFWAY UP the last flight of stairs when Matt's voice greets me, "Whoa. I didn't know today was a shopping-spree day."

"You could help, you know."

"Nah. It's more fun to watch you struggle."

"I swear to God."

He's laughing when he joins me and takes two bags full of shoes and all sorts of other things from my one hand, leaving me with the dress over my arm.

"Thank you. I thought my hand was gonna break."

"Hey, you wanna go on a spree, you've gotta get everything home."

"It wasn't my idea," I groan as we reach the landing and head down the hall. "It was my grandmother's."

"I was gonna say. Bags from Nordstrom. No offense, but that's usually not your style."

"Shopping in an actual, physical store isn't my style either. I'm freaking wiped out." Once we're inside my apartment, I lay the dress in its bag over the back of the sofa before collapsing. "It's so exhausting."

"Oh, I bet. Trying on dresses and shoes, twirling around in a mirror." He leaves the bags by the coffee table and looks down at me with his hands on his hips.

It's a darn shame he's so hot, all tall and muscular and tanned, even in early December, which strikes me as being unfair. He'd make a tasty piece of eye candy if he wasn't such a pain in the butt.

"It wasn't like that at all. My grandmother forced me into it, like I said. I had to try on everything she liked, and it didn't matter if I'd wear it to my own funeral or not. She insisted. No. She ordered."

"Sounds like the apple didn't fall far from the tree." He plunks down in a chair with a smirk.

"I didn't ask you to sit down."

"I carried your bags into your apartment. I think that warrants a few minutes of conversation."

"Yeah, but your idea of conversation usually devolves into making fun of me or making fun of how I'm feeling. Sorry if it doesn't thrill me." I close my eyes with a sigh. "My head hurts."

"What was it all about?"

Oh, he's going to love this. I wish I hadn't run into him. Though he'll find out eventually—the risks of two people who work from home, living across the hall from each other, I guess. We don't have much else to do during the day besides work, so we tend to bug each other.

"She was treating me like a full-grown, living doll, so she can take me to some charity auction this weekend."

"Wow. Your life is so difficult."

"Shut up."

"Seriously, who do you think will play you in the movie they make about your toils and tribulations?"

"I swear to God. When they bring me in for questioning and I'm soaked in your blood, nobody will believe the stuff I tell them. I need to be recording these conversations for future reference."

"Right, but that implies forethought, which wouldn't look good for your defense." He nudges my leg with his foot. "Come on. You know I'm kidding."

"It takes a lot out of me to go shopping. I've never liked it."

"Why not? Especially when there's somebody willing to foot the bill for you—I mean, I assume she did."

"She did, which meant she got final say in what I'm wearing to this event, but that's not what I'm talking about." I sit up with a groan since, jeez, even my body aches.

It's like I went through a session with a trainer, which, let's not lie, my grandmother would be perfect at. So long as she could still look fabulous and sip cocktails while ordering her clients to work harder.

"What are you talking about?" He's not kidding anymore.

One thing I can say about him: he knows when to stop teasing. It hasn't always been this way, but in the months since we've gotten to know each other, he's finally begun to understand my signals. I'm like a cat that can only be tormented for so long before the claws come out.

Which I guess makes Kitty the perfect nickname for me.

"When I was a kid, shopping was stressful. It was almost never fun. Because we didn't have a lot of money, you know?"

He frowns, nodding. "Right. And if I know you, you were always concerned with how much everything cost and whether you were asking for too much."

"How did you come up with that?"

"Like I said, I know you. You have a hard time asking for what you need if you think it'll inconvenience somebody else." He shrugs. "What can I say? I'm a deep thinker."

"You're also full of yourself."

"But I'm not wrong."

"No, you're not wrong. Which is why I like shopping online, not just because it's convenient, but also because I can plan a whole series of looks around a few key pieces, then see what the total in my cart looks like, and pare down if I feel I need to."

He chuckles.

"Hey, sales were low for a while there. My residuals weren't as hefty as they used to be. It's times like that when my frugality comes in handy," I add.

"Fair enough."

"So, you can imagine having to try on these very expensive dresses, which I didn't even like in the first place, which I feel like I don't even need and will probably never have the chance to wear again. It feels wasteful to me. No matter how good life gets, I'm still stuck with those old feelings and patterns. I can't help it."

"Sure you can, if you want to. You have to train your brain to think differently."

I groan and roll my eyes.

"I mean it!" he insists. "I've been reading books about this for a while now. You can borrow them if you want. All about neurology and stuff. You should check them out."

"I don't know that it's that serious."

"You can't only read romance books all the time."

"I don't! I read all genres. It's important for a writer to read widely."

"So, read them. You'll thank me." He eyes the bags. "Anyway, what's the event for?"

"It's an auction to raise money for local animal shelters."

His brows lift. I can tell he's taking me a little

more seriously now, which is miraculous since he almost never does.

"Good cause. I picked up Phoebe at the shelter a few blocks away."

"Really? That beautiful girl was given up?"

Phoebe is a breathtaking golden retriever. There are times when I think I like her a lot more than I like her owner—and considering the fact that she once caused me to sprain my ankle, that's saying something.

"She sure was." A slow smile starts to spread across his generous mouth. "So, what kind of auction is it? Silent auction? Gift baskets and certificates to the spa?"

Here we go. "No."

"Win a date with a romance author?"

"I'm not the one being auctioned off! Oops." I clamp my hands over my mouth as he bursts out laughing.

"Duh. I'm on the email list for the shelter, and it's one of the shelters involved in the event. I already heard all about it."

"Of course." I can never seem to get ahead of him. He always knows just a little more than I do.

"So, is your grandmother that desperate to get you settled down? She'll dress you up and take you out and find a man for you?" He actually has to wipe tears from his eyes by the time he's finished laughing hysterically.

"No, smarty. I have to write about firefighters

this time, and firefighters are being auctioned off."

This kicks off another round of laughter, which, by now, I expect from him. "Oh, that's too good. You have to bid on the guy you think will make the best hero for your next book. What I wouldn't give to be a fly on the wall."

"Hush."

When he doesn't hush, he gets a pillow to the side of his head.

"Seriously! This isn't funny to me. And she offered to foot the bill for my guy, so I guess there's nothing I can do to get out of it."

"Why would you wanna get out of it? It sounds like a perfect setup to me. You don't have to lift a finger aside from getting yourself dressed up and whatnot. All your potential dates are right there in front of you. Like a buffet."

"You're enjoying this way too much."

"Maybe I am."

"Much more than I am."

"Lighten up. You take everything too seriously. It'll be fun if you let it. Imagine how many women will be there, clawing at each other for a date with a lucky bachelor."

Hmm. He might have a point. I wonder how long it'll take before fur starts to fly. If anything, it could be interesting fodder for another book—or even a scene in my current project, which has yet to be started.

"Oh. That could actually be entertaining to

watch."

"See?" He sits back with his hands folded behind his head and a smug grin. "Like I said, I wish I could be a fly on the wall."

"I'll see if I can get some video for you."

Chapter Three

"OH, WHAT A delicious idea! Winning a firefighter in a bachelor auction!" Maggie's pleased as punch when I tell her about this new scheme. "You must write that in your book. You have to. It's perfect."

"I'm already outlining," I promise. "The auction's tonight, so I'll be able to get started soon enough."

"Good to hear since we're salivating over here. As are your readers. They really like the new direction you've taken in your books."

"Well, they're what matters after all."

I have to admit, knowing they're looking forward to reading my next book is thrilling. It's not all about the money. Although it's certainly helpful to have a steady income and be able to continue doing what I love. That's something I'll never take for granted, not after being so unsure whether I'd write another profitable word again.

At the end of the day, I do it for them. The readers. The people who want to escape for a little while into a book, to forget what's going on in real life. I mean, everyday life is sort of a nightmare for a lot of people, for all sorts of reasons. If I can help alleviate that for a little while, so much the better.

And they know what they want, these readers. They're sharp and savvy. And if they don't like what you're putting out there, they'll let you know by refusing to read your books. Not that I know what that feels like or anything.

No. Not me.

"I expect you to look your very best tonight," Maggie crows. "You'll want to make it worth this young man's while."

"I think I can handle it. You realize I know how to go out and be among people, right?"

"Just in case, it never hurts to look your best."

"Of course, of course. But hey, I don't think the guy's going to have much of a choice. When he's mine, he's mine." Grandmother's technically since she's the one paying up. But I don't feel like getting into the particulars with my editor.

"Can I offer advice on the next book since we're already talking about it?"

"I figured this wasn't a social call." I sit back in my chair, crossing my ankles on the coffee table. I just had a pedicure today as well as a manicure. And a facial. And maybe a haircut. Though I didn't go as short as Hayley and Grandmother had wanted. I do have a mind of my own.

"The feedback we've been getting from advance readers is invaluable, and it all points in one direction."

"Let me guess," I sigh.

She doesn't give me a chance. "Hotter. More."

"Right. I get it."

"Don't get me wrong," she insists. "I think what you're writing is head and shoulders above what you wrote before—at least in terms of sex and attraction. You're gifted when it comes to creating chemistry. What we need is heat. Not just chemistry, but also tension. Plenty of it."

"Okay."

She pauses for a beat. "*Just okay*?"

"What else should I say? I've accepted your note, and I'll take it to heart."

"I expected pushback," she admits with a soft laugh. "It seems you've come around nicely."

Come around? More like I've been beaten into submission.

"I have to get better at writing hot sex. Lots of it."

"Yes. And it doesn't always have to happen when the two of them have already decided they like each other a lot. It can happen spontaneously. It can even happen when they hate each other. Hate fucking can be hotter than any other kind really."

Oh, for joy. This is always my favorite part of our talks—when she grants me a glimpse into her personal life. She's an older woman, too, so there's a lot of living under her belt. I have to grit my teeth and roll my eyes and bear it.

"I've never done that," I admit.

"Tell me something else that's supposed to surprise me but doesn't." Her laughter is light, teasing. "You need to find somebody to hate fuck, my young friend."

"I'll make note of that." Then, I have to ask, "What's it like? I mean, don't go into detail, please. But I've always associated sex with emotion as much as with physical attraction. I have to like somebody to want to do it with them. Why would I want to have sex with somebody I hate?"

"Because they're hot and you're hot, and love and hate are often two sides of the same coin. When you truly hate someone—I mean, hate them to the bottom of your soul, to the point where you'd like to see them burn in hell—but you're still attracted to them and you were married for seven years until they cheated on you? It can be very intense when all that hatred boils over."

Gee, I wonder whose personal experiences she's drawing on when she talks about this.

"Okay, I see your point."

"Passion is passion."

"I get it. I do. Thank you."

She's no help though. I have to really understand what it's like to hate somebody while also wanting to have sex with them.

Should I ask Matt?

No. I should definitely not ask Matt. That's possibly the worst thing I could ever do.

Though he's probably the only person in my life who

could offer insight. Darn it.

"Now, get out there tonight and score yourself a hot, sexy firefighter. God, to be young again." She's laughing as she hangs up.

Meanwhile, I feel like I need a shower. And I just took one before she called.

Well, I'm not asking Matt for advice right now; that's for sure.

I have an hour to finish getting ready for the banquet, and knowing Grandmother, she'll notice and comment if I have a single hair out of place.

By the time I'm as ready as I'll ever be, I have to admit, my grandmother has an eye for what suits me. There was no way I'd ever go along with anything she chose for me while we were shopping. I wasn't in the right headspace after trying on a dozen dresses and having each and every one of my problem areas dissected.

Now, days later? I can see why she liked the black dress with its full satin skirt that swishes a little when I move. The bodice is black lace, off the shoulder with long sleeves.

I can still hear her advice. "*You have a beautiful neck and exquisite shoulders. You should show them off.*"

I don't know that my shoulders are exactly exquisite. I mean, they're not weird or misshapen or anything, but exquisite? My hair is up to show them off regardless, and pearls hang around my neck. Grandmother can't be disappointed with me. She'll like showing off her granddaughter.

I hope.

The car is right on time, and the fact that Peter's the one driving both tickles me and concerns me a little.

"Is there anything you don't do for her at all hours of the day and night?" I ask after saying hello.

He only offers a gentle laugh. The man has the patience of a saint.

"What an untoward question." Grandmother looks me up and down once I'm seated and we're on our way to the hotel. "You look lovely, as I knew you would."

"I'll pretend you don't sound smug."

"I know how I sound, and I have every right to. Goodness knows you fought like a toddler who missed their nap while we were shopping."

"I did no such thing."

"Perhaps I'm misremembering. Perhaps I went shopping with another young woman who rolled her eyes and pouted very dramatically every time I asked her to try on something new." She shrugs, sighing.

"I didn't," I huff dramatically. "I rolled my eyes. Maybe."

Peter, meanwhile, is having a good laugh over this whole thing.

"You could back me up a little bit, you know," I grumble his way.

"And you know I would like to defend you, but your grandmother signs my checks." He meets my eyes in the rearview mirror and winks.

I swear, the day he showed up at Grandmother's front door was one of the best days of her life, whether she knows it or not.

I turn to my grandmother, who looks like a million bucks and is even wearing a cape. An actual cape with a collar encrusted in pearls. She might as well be a queen on her throne.

Maybe the sight of her looking so regal and dignified and the reminder of the whole signing-checks thing—in other words, the fact that she's paying for all of this—are what soften my attitude. "Thank you for this. I know I was a little difficult at the store, but this means a lot."

"That's more like it. Honestly, you do someone a favor, and they treat you like a villain."

I would hardly say I treated her like a villain. The next time Hayley asks where I got my dramatic streak from, I'll point her in grandmother's direction. "Anyway, do you know how many people are supposed to be there tonight?"

"The last time I checked, we sold two hundred fifty tickets. And there are two dozen bachelors up for auction."

"Two dozen? How will I know which one to pick?" The second it's out of my mouth, the corners of her mouth twitch upward, like she's trying to hide a smile. "No. Don't tell me you've already chosen someone for me."

"Why would I not? I had the luxury of vetting

these young men, and several of them stood out above the rest."

"Excuse me, but maybe I should've been given that luxury? Did you ever think of that? I'm the one who's supposed to be dating him."

"Yes, and we've seen how well you've done in the past when left to your own devices." Before I have the chance to come up with a cutting reply, she pats my hand. "I understand. You're not looking for anything serious or long-term. Still, there are times when we must admit we can't see the big picture. It's always easier for someone standing outside our situation to see what we can't because we are too close to it."

I hate it when she's right, though it would have been nice to be alerted to this information. I mean, I could've already picked out who I wanted. "I think I'm the one who should have been able to check them out regardless. I'm supposed to be writing a book about this person."

She holds up a finger, clicking her tongue. "A book inspired by them. I thought the point was to use them for inspiration."

Darn it. There are times I wish I didn't tell her so much of what goes on in my professional life. "Okay, you're making a point, but still, I don't like feeling like I have no say in the matter."

"Would it help if I told you I think you'll be pleased?"

"Not very much."

"Kathryn, give me at least a small bit of credit. I have good taste in men. Your grandfather—rest his soul—was a regular stud."

"Oh God."

Her blithe shrug nearly ends me. "Well? He was."

"It's just that I don't need to hear that, you know?"

"I swear, if I had a dollar for every morning I woke up, unable to walk …"

"Oh, here we are!" I've never been so glad to see a hotel in all my life. It's a good thing we didn't get stuck in traffic or else I might've been treated to the story of how my mother was conceived.

Grandmother is clearly having the time of her life, tormenting me, chuckling to herself as Peter gets out of the car to help her from the backseat. I slide over and take his outstretched hand. If anything, that slight contact gives me a boost, makes me feel a little less like I'm about to walk into a lion's den. I'm not even one of the people being auctioned off, but knowing that doesn't stop my hands from shaking a little.

"You know she means well," Peter whispers while Grandmother greets a friend on her way into the hotel. "You're the only family she has, and it means a great deal to see you settled down and content. That's all she wants."

Part of me wants to ask how he knows this. I doubt the two of them sit around, sharing their private thoughts over a cup of tea before heading to bed. But he has been with her a long time, and I guess he's been able to pick up a few things here and there.

Reaching up, I pat his wrinkled cheek. "I've said it before, and I'll say it again. There are times I'm sure you're what I like best about her."

Grandmother turns when she realizes I'm not with her. "Kathryn! Come along. It won't do for us to be late."

"As if she doesn't love making an entrance after everyone else has arrived." I wink at Peter before hurrying to catch up with her, and his laughter follows me up to the gilded front door.

It's time for Grandmother to buy me a man. I'm not saying it's the worst way I've ever spent a Saturday night, but still …

Chapter Four

My FIRST THOUGHTS on entering the ballroom on the top floor of the hotel have nothing to do with the beautiful surroundings, the impeccable floral arrangements, the ornate gold-and-crystal chandeliers hanging from the ceiling painted with fluffy clouds against a blue sky.

No, my thoughts have more to do with the feeling of being a kid in a candy store.

There are so many gorgeous men here; I don't know where to look first. Sure, the women are beautiful and exquisitely dressed, but it's the men wearing badges designating them as firefighters participating in the auction who catch my eye and get my imagination moving.

I'm not the only one impressed, not by a long shot. I don't think I've ever seen so many women twirl their hair around their fingers while laughing loudly and smacking a man's arm in one place. Honestly, it's like they're holding a flirting convention.

Only it would have to be a convention to teach people how to flirt because some of what I'm seeing as Grandmother weaves me through the ballroom is downright cringeworthy.

"Whitney! You look fabulous."

Grandmother and her frenemy, Whitney, exchange air kisses before Whitney takes notice of me. Immediately, her eyes light up, and I know why. She practically mauled Jake, the doctor I dated for one of my books, during grandmother's seventy-fifth birthday party.

"Kathryn! You are a vision." I get the same air-kiss treatment before she looks around behind me. "Where is that gorgeous doctor of yours?"

Grandmother swoops in before I get the chance to speak for myself. "I'm sorry to say, that didn't work out."

If Whitney could move a muscle on her face, I'm sure she would be frowning. But there's a reason she looks so good for a woman her age, and a lot of it has to do with how immobile her face is. Not that I knock it—people should be able to do what they want with their faces and their bodies—but there's a certain point where a woman starts to look like she's wearing a mask that only vaguely resembles her.

Whitney passed that point a few treatments ago.

"I'm so sorry to hear that. Goodness, he was something else." She fans herself. "I can only imagine what he must've been like in bed."

All I can do is give her a nervous laugh. "Me too." I shrug before gladly accepting a glass of champagne from a passing server. I have a feeling tonight is going to be the sort of event that requires a lot of alcohol.

It's a relief when somebody calls Whitney away to handle something. I can slightly exhale—but not for long.

"I need to speak to a few of the organizers," Grandmother informs me. "By all means, mingle."

"But …"

It's too late. She moves much faster than a woman of her age should be able to. One second, she was standing next to me, and the next, she's blended into the crowd, to the point where I can't make her out.

Terrific.

Well, she wanted me to mingle. So, I do, wandering in and out of small groups, exchanging pleasantries. There are plenty of women here around my age, and I can feel a sense of excitement from them. Well, of course they're excited. They're here to bid on men.

And to help homeless dogs and cats, obviously. Naturally, that's all any of us really care about.

Actually, I care more about something else right now. And it's not my book. It's the heavenly aroma of various appetizers being carried around on silver trays. I'm so stinking hungry. I should have eaten something before leaving. Come to think of it, I should've eaten something more than a banana this morning before going to get my nails done. I sort of forgot to eat.

Here's the thing: I know myself. And I know that this champagne is going to go straight to my head if I don't put something in my stomach. Which is why, when a tray of stuffed mushrooms floats past on the hand of a server, I grab one at the last second and pop it into my mouth.

And I instantly regret it because they must've just come straight from the kitchen. I open my mouth and do that frantic exhale thing people do when they're trying to cool something that's already crossed their tongue. That doesn't work, so I have no choice but to wave my hand in front of my mouth before downing another glass of champagne. That finally does the trick.

Of course, I looked super classy and elegant the entire time I did that. And I'm sure the few people standing nearby who were watching feel that way. I give them a little wave and a shrug, and they barely manage to avoid rolling their eyes before turning away to continue their conversation.

Someone clears their throat behind me. "Gotta be careful about those hot appetizers."

Oh no. No, no, no. Please, God, not tonight. Of all nights, don't let that voice belong to the person I think it belongs to.

I don't even want to turn around. Because if I turn around and find that the person behind me is indeed my neighbor, I'll …

Okay, I don't know what I'll do. But it won't be

pretty.

"Did you go deaf? Did that stuffed mushroom make you go deaf?" Rather than waiting for me to turn around and face him, Matt sidles up beside me and gently nudges me with his elbow. "How's your mouth?"

How's my mouth? It sort of feels like I swallowed poison.

I turn to him, brows raised. "Could you maybe have told me you were planning on coming here tonight? I mean, we did talk about this event."

He shrugs, grinning. "We were talking about you, not me."

"Don't give me that. You know what I'm saying. You had a chance to mention you were coming here tonight. Why didn't you?"

He waves a hand at me. "Because of this. Because I didn't need you to give me an attitude. Sorry, but I had already bought my ticket. It was a done deal before you announced you were coming."

I bat my eyelashes at him. "Oh, really? Looking to bid on a bachelor?"

"Yes, I realized my apartment was missing something. A single firefighter would look just great. Maybe he can sleep next to Phoebe's crate."

I have to laugh. "Well, you clean up nicely anyway."

Okay, that's a huge understatement. He looks absolutely incredible. I mean, he's hot enough in regular clothes.

The man is wearing a tuxedo tonight. It fits him like a glove. His hair, which is usually a little unkempt—one of the many perks of working at home, I guess—is neatly trimmed and smoothed down.

"Thanks. So do you." He raises his champagne glass to me, eyes moving up and down to take me in. "Your grandmother has good taste even if yours is sometimes questionable."

"Shut up."

Then, I see an older woman approaching us. I don't remember her name, but I recognize her from Grandmother's birthday party.

I could be anybody in the entire world as far as she's concerned. In fact, I doubt she would notice if she stepped on me since she only has eyes for Matt.

"Now, now, let's not monopolize our bachelors." She scarcely glances at me, too busy looking up at Matt with adoring eyes.

He dazzles her with a bright smile. "I'm flattered, but I'm not one of the bachelors up for auction tonight. Though I'm pretty good with a fire extinguisher."

Honestly, when he's out in public, he knows how to turn on the charm. He almost passes for a human being.

"Oh, come on. I'm sure they can squeeze in one more handsome young man." She finally looks at me, and I can tell she vaguely recognizes me, just like I vaguely recognize her. "Come on. Help me convince him."

Help her convince him?

Oh, yes. I would like nothing more.

I look up at him with big, innocent eyes that are anything but truly innocent. "She's right, Matt. You're here tonight, which means the shelter is important to you. Just imagine the money you could help raise to save other dogs like Phoebe. Just think, there could be dogs just like her right now, waiting for someone to come and love them."

"She's so right," Grandmother's friend coos, patting Matt's arm.

"He'd probably bring in a lot of money too, wouldn't he?" I ask her while he basically burns up with embarrassment. I can practically feel the heat coming off him in waves.

I'm not an idiot. I know he's going to make me pay for this. But it'll be worth it because I'll always have this memory of making him blush to the roots of his hair. I'm surprised his teeth aren't blushing when he forces a tight smile.

"I don't know if I qualify."

"You're single," I say to him. "He's single," I assure the woman who's now definitely taking exploratory squeezes of Matt's bicep. I've seen that bicep without clothes covering it up. I know how impressive it is. "And he has a great job too. He's a catch and a half."

"I will kill you," he mutters out of the side of his

mouth while smiling to the woman in front of him.

"You can try," I mutter back, also smiling.

"Don't make me bring my friends over here to convince you," the woman warns, shaking a bejeweled finger at him. "They are very convincing when they want to be."

"By all means, bring them over." Especially since one of them happens to be my grandmother. "Better yet, let's go join them." I link arms with Matt and pull him along with me, which is much easier said than done since he's doing his darnedest to plant his feet.

"You are so gonna pay for this," he whispers while we wind our way through the crowd, finally reaching my grandmother and Whitney and the few friends they're chatting with.

"Grandmother! My friend and neighbor is here. Matt Ryder, meet my grandmother." I might or might not give him a tiny shove to make sure he gets closer.

Boy, she's good. She looks him up and down with one of her practiced eye flicks while extending a hand. "Any friend of Kathryn's. What brings you here tonight?"

"Kathryn is trying to convince him to add his name to our roster of bachelors." Her friend holding on to Matt now, nearly leaning on him. "Don't you think that's a good idea?"

Now, all eyes are on us, and maybe this has gone too far.

I clear my throat and shrug. "I don't know. It was just an idea. He certainly doesn't have to do anything he's not comfortable with."

He looks down at me, brow furrowed. What's he thinking? Probably trying to decide if I mean it or not.

Then, he smiles, and my insides turn to ice. I can see he's cooking up some scheme in the back of his mind, to get back at me. And he's latched on to something.

"No, that's fine. If there's room for me, I'd be more than happy to offer myself as a bachelor." He shines the light of his smile on everyone around us. "Not that I want to rock the boat, mind you, but I did adopt my dog from one of the shelters receiving proceeds from tonight's auction, so it means a lot to me."

I swear, every one of the women around me— besides Grandmother—is ready to swoon.

She's not quite there yet. "You would have to provide a bit of biographical information."

"Fair enough."

"And you'll have to accept a date with whichever woman wins you during bidding."

"Also fair." He shrugs a little, looking around. "You're more than welcome to say no. This wasn't my idea."

"There are already two dozen, aren't there? Do we really need one more?" I whisper to my grandmother as the others murmur among themselves.

"If he's been generous enough to accept, it would be wrong to turn him down now." Grand-mother clearly has the last word in just about everything, including the etiquette used by her social circle. "Yes, I think that's a fine idea. The more, the merrier."

Matt's smile widens when his eyes meet mine.

Boy, am I in for it.

Chapter Five

IT TAKES ALL of my concentration to turn my thoughts toward the auction and away from the fact that Matt's going to exact cruel and relentless punishment after I threw him under the bus. Even the sumptuous-looking dinner in front of me—chateaubriand, scalloped potatoes, roasted brussels sprouts with bacon, which smells absolutely divine—tastes like sawdust in my mouth.

I feel bad. What can I say?

And darn him for taking away the opportunity to get to know a few of the bachelors. Just like Matt, monopolizing my time and leaving me feeling like the bad guy.

"Dear? Did you hear a word I said?" Grandmother stops short of waving a hand in front of my face but just barely.

"Hmm? I'm sorry. I didn't."

We're seated near the front of the room, next to the catwalk where all the men will strut their stuff, so I have to keep a pleasant smile on my face for the sake of people looking this way. I'm sure everybody would love to report that Cecile's granddaughter looked like she needed an exorcism at the big fundraiser.

"I said, the bachelor in question is thirteenth on the list. Keep your eyes open."

"Thirteenth? Not a lucky number."

"Oh, don't be silly." She waves a hand with a soft laugh. "As if that sort of thing truly matters. Really, Kathryn. You haven't touched your dinner either."

Only the fact that we're in public and around a bunch of fancy, rich people keeps me from poking my meat just to prove I touched it. Instead of doing something truly juvenile, I pick up my knife and fork and cut into the beef.

Anybody who wonders why it took me so long to dig in can tell themselves I was nervous about the auction.

Or they can mind their own business if it actually matters enough for them to think about it.

Whitney calls out to me from across the table, "Kathryn, darling, will you be bidding on any of the bachelors?"

Grandmother sees fit to respond for me, "She will."

"Yes, I will." I turn to my grandmother. "Wow, I've gotten so good at throwing my voice without even trying to."

"Careful, or you won't be bidding on anyone. Remember, you're here, thanks to my generosity."

"Of course. You're right." And I have to write a

book, which means I need a firefighter. I only wish I could've picked my own, is all. But beggars can't be choosers.

Especially when the opening bid on the first bachelor—a tall, hunky ginger who likes skiing and rock climbing—is a thousand dollars.

I mean, he's a complete meal. Not a snack. A meal.

He strides down the catwalk, and I realize I've forgotten to breathe.

But a thousand dollars? To start? I'm way out of my league here.

"What a hunk!" Whitney fans herself as he walks past. "To be young again."

Funny, that's the second time I've heard that today.

"I would never expect you to let a little thing like age get in the way," I tease.

"Well, no. But still." She's having too much fun, openly ogling the eye candy onstage.

Meanwhile, the bidding has reached four thousand dollars and is still climbing.

"Come on, ladies. It's for a great cause, you know." The emcee is loving this, her voice heavy with deeper meaning. "And you get a night with a hot firefighter out of it too. Also a great cause."

Finally, he goes for just over four thousand, to much applause. The next bachelor takes his turn, and the next.

"Holy smokes—no pun intended," I whisper to

Grandmother. "I had no idea there were so many gorgeous firefighters in this city."

I can understand them being fit, naturally. Their job is physically demanding.

But they're so handsome too. Square jaws abound, as do pouty lips and deep-set eyes and just the right amount of scruff on their cheeks.

"We took the liberty of hiring a stylist for tonight," Grandmother admits with a tiny wince. "Just to be sure the men looked their best."

"Well, you did a darn good job. I wish I could bid on all of them."

"If you do, it'll be with your own money, my dear."

She's waiting on number thirteen. So am I, especially considering how eligible and panty-melting the men I've seen so far happen to be.

"You're sure you picked the best bachelor? Because I could go for number ten up there." I can't take my eyes off this one.

He's a Nordic god come to life—tall, blond, his eyes so piercingly blue that they practically stop my heart when they lock with mine before he continues down the catwalk.

"Fifteen hundred!" Whitney calls out, waving her little paddle thingy in the air to signal a bid.

"Whitney!" Grandmother laughs while I gape at her in awe.

"What? He's gorgeous! And I'm sure he wouldn't mind a lovely meal at a fine restaurant."

Whitney shrugs at us. "It's for charity. I do what I can."

"Yes, you're a regular saint." At least Grandmother manages to keep from rolling her eyes until Whitney's already turned away because another bidder offered seventeen hundred, right away followed by another offer of eighteen hundred.

I wonder what it's like for the men, standing up there, waiting to be won. They're used to working hard, saving lives and doing what many people don't have the strength to do or dare to even attempt.

And here they are in tuxedos, at an event that cost hundreds of dollars to attend.

The Nordic god goes for twenty-five hundred. Not bad. Easily one of the top earners of the night so far. Number eleven goes for twenty-two hundred. Twelve goes for twenty-eight hundred after a pair of eager bidders went toe-to-toe from across the room, shouting new bids rapid-fire.

I could write an entire book about this. It's supposed to be in fun, yet there's a definite competitive streak in these women. Maybe they're used to getting what they want. Maybe some of these bidding wars have to do with personal issues between them. It's a big city, New York, but the upper crust is a smaller world of its own.

Grandmother clicks her tongue in disdain when the winning bidder raises her hands in victory. I know that sound well. "Veronica Jordan. Classless, just like her mother."

Good thing I just swallowed a mouthful of water or else I might've spit it out all over the table.

Someday, I need to get Grandmother tipsy and pick her brain. Maybe I should be tipsy at the time, come to think of it, since I'm sure some of what would come out of her mouth would scandalize me.

"Now, ladies and gentlemen, we move on to bachelor thirteen."

I sit up straighter and remind myself to breathe. *This is it. This is my bachelor.* "I'm trusting you," I whisper to Grandmother before the emcee announces my fella's name.

"Bachelor thirteen is Bryce Nichols, and he hails from Brooklyn."

Okay, good start. We have something in common.

Wait.

Bryce Nichols.

I know that name.

And I know the face as Bryce steps out onstage. Yes, time has passed. Yes, his boyish good looks have sharpened into something downright devastating. There's no more baby fat in those flat cheeks, no crookedness in his teeth.

I wonder if he grew out of the habit of being a heartless bully in the last fifteen years.

"No." I lean over and nudge Grandmother. Hard. "No, not him. Son of a—"

"What is wrong with you?" She sighs, clearly exasperated, while my middle-school bully strides down the catwalk.

"He made my life hell in middle school; that's what's wrong with me. No way. I'm not dating him."

"Come on now." She turns to me with another sigh. "You're both adults. I chose him because he hails from Brooklyn, as do you. He's well-educated and a decorated Navy veteran, and he was awarded for saving two children from their home during a fire this past summer. He's the perfect catch for you."

All that, and he's only two years older than me.

I have a hard time believing the man striding down the catwalk is the man Grandmother is describing. All I see is the absolute nightmare who made fun of everything about me in middle school. Thankfully, it was only one year since he's older than me.

But the fact that I remember that year so clearly should say something. Because it was torment. And I wasn't the only person he bullied either. He had a bad reputation around school for pantsing boys in the locker room and shoving kids into closets and blocking the door so they couldn't get out. He was once suspended for tripping a kid and sending him falling down a short flight of stairs.

That was near the end of the school year, and I think he might've learned his lesson after that because it's the last thing I remember hearing about.

But I can't believe he's changed that much. Bullies don't magically stop being bullies. They can do good things at work and still push smaller, weaker people around on their downtime.

"We'll start the bidding at one thousand dollars," the emcee announces while Bryce stands next to her with a relaxed, easy sort of posture and a wry grin.

Yeah, I just bet he thinks this is amusing.

He runs a hand over his black hair, sort of playing at primping himself, and the women seated around the catwalk laugh.

I don't laugh. I'm pretty sure what comes out is more like a snarl.

"One thousand!"

"Eleven hundred!"

"Twelve fifty!"

"Kathryn, bid on him." Grandmother shoots me a dirty look. "Now."

"I won't." I sit back, arms folded, glaring at the man onstage. No freaking way am I sharing air with him for longer than I absolutely have to.

"Kathryn."

"Nope. He used to spit on me. He gave me a complex. It took me ages to get over it." Clearly, I never quite finished getting over it because the sight of him makes me sick.

Meanwhile, the bidding's up to two thousand dollars, and it doesn't seem like there's any slowing down. Grandmother isn't the only one who thinks Bryce is the total package.

"Bid on him, Kathryn," she hisses.

"I can't. Anybody else. Not him. Please." I even fold my hands, begging. "I used to have stomach-aches, just thinking about seeing him in school. I used to get demerits for being late to class, all because I was hiding from him in the hallway beforehand. He made me feel ugly and small."

She's got to understand that, right? The woman is my grandmother, for Pete's sake, and she at least puts on a good act of loving me.

"Twenty-five hundred!" She turns to the emcee, pointing to me. "For my granddaughter."

"I can't believe this," I whisper, humiliated. My cheeks feel like they're on fire.

Matt would wet his pants with laughter if he knew what was happening out here, but he's backstage, waiting his turn. One small point of light in this otherwise dismal situation.

"Twenty-five hundred," the emcee echoes with a grin.

"Twenty-six!"

"Twenty-seven fifty!"

"Think of it this way." Grandmother turns to me, and I brace myself for a tongue-lashing. "How much would you pay to tell him what you think of him? How much would it be worth to you? To finally set things straight? To tell him everything he did and how it made you feel? To take notes on his work life for your book because, damn it, he owes you that much after tormenting you for an entire year? What would that be worth?" That was not what I was expecting her to say.

Oh.

Oh, that's different.

"Three thousand!" I shout.

Yes, he's going to tell me what I want to know—after I give him a hearty piece of my mind.

Grandmother sits back with a satisfied smile. "That's my girl."

"Thirty-two!"

"Thirty-three!"

"Thirty-five hundred!" I look at my grandmother to make sure I'm not going too far.

She only nods and raises her champagne glass.

Yes, I'm gonna get my man.

Chapter Six

FIVE THOUSAND THREE hundred dollars.

Evidently, that's what it costs for the opportunity to give somebody an earful. To set the record straight. To get a little bit of my own back. Over five thousand dollars.

By the time the bidding's over and I've won my bully, who happens to be a firefighter—I need to keep that in mind since it's sort of the entire reason we're doing this—there's nothing to do but sit back and catch my breath.

Whitney shoots me an appraising look from across the table. "Well, you were determined."

"I was."

"I'm surprised you didn't stand on the chair."

"Whitney," Grandmother warns with narrowed eyes. "When my granddaughter knows what she wants, she goes after it. Much like her grandmother."

"Point taken." She's still a little too smirky when she turns away though.

Now, all that's left to do is wait for the rest of the bachelors to be auctioned off. The one bright spot in this is when it comes time for Matt to be auctioned.

"Ladies, ladies, don't fret if you haven't yet landed the man of your dreams."

I sit up at attention and try like heck to fight back a smile. If I'm going to suffer for this—and I know I will—I might as well enjoy Matt's discomfort.

"We have a surprise for you. No, he isn't a firefighter," the emcee announces, "but he is an investment manager from right here in Manhattan, who enjoys going for runs in the park with his shelter dog, Phoebe. When he isn't managing high-value portfolios for his clients from the comfort of his Upper West Side apartment, he enjoys reading, going to concerts, and getting to know the delivery drivers from his favorite takeout restaurants."

That last quip earns a laugh from the women around me. Even I have to chuckle, though to be fair, he should've added the part where he used to piggyback off my orders and save himself the delivery fee. The cheap jerk.

When he saunters onto the stage, I'm pretty sure I could hear a pin drop, if any happened to get dropped. The room might as well be empty; it goes so quiet for a split second.

But only for that split second. Matt hardly needs to step out onto the catwalk before the bidding begins.

Now, I could tell myself this is nothing more

than an act of last-minute desperation on the part of the women who have been bidding their hearts out and ending up with nothing to show for it.

I could more truthfully tell myself there are women out here who love the idea of dating a guy who works with money and numbers. The firefighters are gorgeous and hot and everything, but they're only supposed to be going on one date with the women who won them—which is probably just fine from the perspective of the winners since I can't imagine these snobs settling into a relationship with a man who swallows smoke for a living.

But Matt? He's a different story. He lives on the Upper West Side and works with money. And he happens to be drop-dead gorgeous. He's a catch.

"Two thousand!"

"Twenty-five hundred!"

"Three thousand!"

"Holy crap." I have to shake my head in wonder as the bids overlap, to the point where one voice is practically indistinguishable from another. "He knew this was going to happen, the creep."

"He's gorgeous." Grandmother turns to me, arching one eyebrow. "And he's your neighbor, you say?"

"He lives across the hall."

"Oh goodness. How do you manage to get any writing done with that across the hall?"

"I do what I can," I growl as the bids go up and up.

"I would ask him for a cup of sugar anytime," Whitney purrs, watching him walk up and down while the dollar amount gets higher. "How do you not get pregnant just by looking at him?"

Oh my God, can this be over?

By the time the bidders hit five thousand dollars, Matt finds me. And darned if he doesn't look like the cat that ate the cream when our eyes meet and his smile widens. The snide, arrogant—

"Sold for seventy-five hundred dollars!" Even the emcee has to applaud at the final total, which is way more than anybody else has earned.

In fact, Bryce is the second-highest-earning bachelor tonight, and there's more than a two-thousand-dollar gap in between.

Maybe I'll get lucky, and this is the only revenge Matt planned when he agreed to do this.

Maybe I'll step outside to find pigs flying down Fifty-Fifth Street.

Grandmother turns to me with a triumphant smile. "What a success! Just think of all those animals that will have better living conditions as they wait to be adopted."

Yes, that's definitely what I'm thinking about. Not about how Matt's going to remind me at least twice a day that he earned seventy-five hundred bucks tonight. And most certainly not about how Bryce Nichols once waited for me outside the girls' restroom door and then tripped me on my way out, which made my skirt fly up, revealing my underwear to everybody in the hallway.

Nope. Not thinking about that at all.

"Ladies, be sure to flag down your lucky bachelor, so the two of you can get to know each other!"

Oh, I'll be doing that. No worries there.

"Now, now," Grandmother warns when I stand. "Try not to flay him in public. At least, not while you're around people I know."

"I'll do my best."

Where is he? I scan the room, looking for his stupid, punchable face. Oh, the nights I spent fantasizing about how wonderful it would be to punch him. Hard. Until he bled. Sometimes, I did it when it was just the two of us, alone. Sometimes, it was in front of a packed auditorium.

No matter the circumstances, it always gave me a tiny bit of satisfaction to imagine doing it.

Now, when his face is much better than it used to be? Oh, the joy of ruining it.

"Excuse me? Aren't you the woman who placed the winning bid for me?"

I turn around fast enough to knock myself off-balance, and a pair of strong hands holds me up.

"Easy there. I didn't mean to startle you."

Looking up, I find a pair of warm brown eyes. I wonder how they'd look if they were swollen. Because of my fists.

"A little too much champagne, I guess." I shake his hands off with a laugh. "It's funny actually, that you should help me stay on my feet."

He doesn't recognize me. It's clear from the confusion washing across his annoyingly perfect, symmetric features. "Pardon?"

"I mean, you spent an entire year tripping me and shoving me around, so ..." I shrug, laughing again. Enjoying the way he squirms.

"I'm sorry. I don't remember you—though I was a real idiot when I was a kid, so I don't doubt that I made your life difficult at one time or another." He offers a wince and a shrug. Like that makes up for anything.

"I'm Kitty Valentine. You know, the only *kitty* you wouldn't touch on a dare? I didn't understand what that meant when I was eleven years old, but now, I get it."

His eyes widen. His jaw drops. "Kitty! Oh my God. Oh, Kitty, I am so sorry. Jesus, I was cruel to you."

"No kidding. At least you can be honest about it. Most bullies pretend what they did was no big deal."

"I'm not pretending." He puts a hand to his chest, which I must admit looks impressively broad. "I mean it. I used to think about you sometimes and wonder what happened to you, honest to God. I was beyond cruel. I was a real prick."

Is he for real? I don't know how to act. I was sure he'd laugh this off or act like it was nothing but kid stuff. "You were."

"Now, I feel terrible. I should have been the one

bidding on taking you out for the night. I owe you a lot more than that in fact." He shakes his head, rubbing one hand over the back of his neck. "I can't apologize enough. But I can try to make it up to you. What do you say?"

What do I say? I say, I wish he would act like a bully, so I can feel justified in treating him like one. Now, I sort of feel like a jerk myself, my chest puffed out and my arms folded when he's being nothing but kind.

Yes, but Dustin acted kind too. He treated me like I was the only woman in the world. Really, all he wanted was a quick lay and publicity from having his name in one of my books. Looks can be deceptive.

"I think I know how you can make it up to me," I inform.

"Really? What can I do?"

Darn it, he looks so contrite, his thick brows pulled together over the bridge of his nose, his mouth turned down at the corners.

"You can help me with a book I need to write. About a firefighter. That's the reason I'm here. To meet a firefighter and learn about his work, so I can use that information for my next book. My grandmother insisted I bid on you," I add at the end because, obviously, there were twenty-three other men to choose from and there was no other reason I absolutely had to choose him.

He blinks, staring at me. "I'm a little confused."

"It's a long story, which I guess we can get into another time. Like when we get together."

One problem: now that I have him, I don't know what to do with him. This would be awkward enough if he was a complete stranger.

All I can think of is how to avoid making myself look like a dork. I can't help it. I'm used to him searching for the weakest point and going for it, guns blazing. I'm used to him taking advantage of any little slip of the tongue.

"That would be great. I'd love the chance to get to know you now. I never had the chance before, and I was always sorry for that." He rubs the back of his neck again with a wry grin. "You'll think I'm lying when I say this, but I actually had a crush on you back then."

"You're right. I do think you're lying."

"Fair enough." He holds out a hand between us. "Let's start from the beginning, huh? I'm Bryce. I'm a New York City firefighter. I would like to get to know you. Over dinner maybe? What do you think?"

I think that when he smiles, I can almost forget how miserable he made me. How he used to make the other kids laugh at me. He's going to have to work pretty hard to get in my good graces.

"I think you should let me know when you're free. I'm sure your schedule is different from mine." Instead of shaking his hand, I press a slip of paper into it. "My number. I look forward to learning more about what you do for a living."

His smile falters but only a little. "Fair enough again. I'll give you a call on Monday after my schedule is posted. Sound good?"

"Sure. And, um, it's nice of you to help raise money for the shelters." That's all I allow myself to say right now. "See you soon."

Yes, it's better for me to get out of here now since I don't trust myself and I need to get my head on straight. Four glasses of champagne don't mix well with a hefty dose of surprise and a sprinkling of childhood humiliation.

Chapter Seven

"SOMETHING GREASY, PLEASE." It's a struggle to keep my head off the table the morning after the auction.

Hayley's in much better shape than I am, but that's nothing new. It's pretty much on-brand for our friendship really. "She'll have two eggs fried over easy, bacon, hash browns, and rye toast with butter."

"Yeah, that sounds about right." A sip of my mimosa makes the world feel a little less brutal. Hair of the dog and all that. But I won't have more than one. In fact, I might never drink another mimosa for as long as I live. Champagne isn't worth the morning after.

When we're alone, she shakes her head at me. "Okay, now that we're together, explain what the heck that rambling voice mail was all about last night. I could barely make out half of it."

"Sorry. I was a little upset."

"A little? You were ranting so fast that all your words ran together. I was thinking you'd at least be in a decent mood today. Scoring a hunky firefighter."

"I scored one. He's hunky—I'll give him that much." I can't keep her in suspense forever, so I open up and share exactly who Bryce is and what he means to me.

By the time I'm finished, our food has arrived.

Hayley barely glances down at it even though she was starving just a few minutes ago. "You bid on your bully?"

"It wasn't my idea!"

"Didn't they have, you know, a booklet or something with information on the bachelors up for auction?"

Whoops. "I don't know." I sink a little in my seat. "Maybe. I was too busy with stupid Matt."

"Matt? What's he got to do with anything? I swear, I let you go out without me just one freaking time, and look what happens."

I have to catch her up on that as I plow through the enormous platter she ordered for me. "Go with the grits instead of potatoes next time," I advise when I'm finished filling her in.

"Yeah, will do. So, wait. Matt was one of the bachelors?"

"Yep."

Her laughter rings out, making a few of our fellow diners look our way. She ignores them, which she's very good at doing. "And he made all that money for the shelters? He'll never let you live it down."

"You don't have to tell me that. Believe me, I'm

already bracing myself for what I know is coming." I pick up a piece of toast. "No butter on the toast next time either. I like to make a bacon sandwich with the toast, but if there's already butter on it …"

"Right, right. So, you were too busy setting Matt up, which means you were too busy setting yourself up, to check out who the bachelors were before the auction started."

"Yeah. I didn't even think about it, to be honest. Grandmother said she had everything under control. I didn't like it, but how was I supposed to know the one she'd chosen was the bane of my childhood?"

"Just think, you dated your dream crush, and now, you'll date the person who made you miserable around the same time. It's like you're coming full circle."

"I wish I had a best friend who supported me. I truly do."

"Come on …"

"Somebody who'd sympathize and tell me it's not my fault fate has a hard-on for me."

"Kitty!" She almost chokes on her French toast.

"I'm serious. Last night, I was fired up and more than a little buzzed. I couldn't wait to tear into him. That was before I spoke to him face-to-face."

"What happened?"

"He was nice!" I throw my hands in the air.

"Oh no!" Hayley giggles. "How dare he be nice!"

"You don't get it. I expected him to be mean. Or to laugh it off like it was all a joke and that I needed to get over it. I expected him to at least remind me how much time had passed. But he remembered me. He was sorry. I mean, it seemed like he was legitimately sorry. Not fake sorry."

"What a monster."

"You're no help."

She laughs, gently kicking me under the table. "I'm sorry. Really. That must've been such a shock, seeing him. Like being dropped in an icy pool with no warning."

"That's exactly how it felt. I might as well have been eleven years old again. Not in a good way. He used to humiliate me. I couldn't do anything right. I never did know why."

"Maybe he was just a sociopathic kid who received treatment."

"You can't treat a sociopath. It doesn't work that way." I chew on a piece of toast, thinking it over. "You know, he even said he had a crush on me back then."

"What?" It's a shriek. An absolute shriek.

"Sorry," I whisper to the people around us, who are none too thrilled with my bestie at the moment. It's usually me who attracts negative attention when I do things like that. This is almost refreshing.

She ignores them again in favor of leaning across the table. "So, he said he had a crush on you back then? That was why he tormented you?"

"How lame, right? Like, the oldest story in the book."

"But it's been known to happen or else it wouldn't be the oldest story. Somebody, at some time, had a crush on somebody else and didn't know what to do about it. So, they teased the person they had the crush on."

"This wasn't teasing. And it's not like I'm the only person he ever bullied. The kid got suspended for it once."

"Yikes."

"I'm glad social media wasn't such a thing back then, or he would've made my life miserable both in and out of school. I swear, I don't know how kids do it nowadays."

"We're careening off-topic." She folds her hands, very businesslike. "What we have here is a case of a man who could very well have grown up and out of the whole bullying thing over the years you haven't known him. You said he was a veteran. We know he's a firefighter. I mean, this speaks well for him."

"True."

"And there's been a lot of time for a person to grow and mature since then."

"Also true."

"Didn't you ever do anything back then that you'd never think of doing now?"

I roll my eyes. "Hayley, this is hardly the same as looking up dirty words on the internet."

"You know what I mean. I say, give him a chance. And even if this goes no further than a single date, make sure you get everything you need out of him before it's over. All the information, all the terms you need to know. Get him to tell you stories and take notes, if you have to, right in front of him. For once, you're going out with a man who knows from the get-go why you're dating him."

"That's true. It'll be easier to do what I need since he already knows why I'm going on this date in the first place. I don't have to worry about hurting his feelings or having him think I'm using him."

"If anything, he deserves to have his feelings hurt a little."

"Also true."

"But I know you. You're not the sort of person to hurt somebody's feelings on purpose."

"I think you're wrong about me."

"I'm not. You're a good person. You're sweet and loving and considerate when you aren't throwing dramatic fits."

"Thanks, I think?"

"You'll want to hurt him, but you won't. It's not in your nature. You'll be snarky, of course, because you're good at that. But in the end, you'll let it go. You'll get all the information you need, and you'll write a best seller. Because that's what you do."

"It doesn't seem right."

"What doesn't?"

"Letting him get away without punishing him somehow. He deserves it. I'm serious," I insist when Hayley shakes her head. "He made me cry. He humiliated me. I wanted to switch schools because of him."

"And I'm really, truly, deeply sorry that happened to you. Hey!" She brightens up like somebody flipped a switch and turned on the lights. "I know! You should write about that. Maybe do a bully romance. That's popular right now, you know."

"So I've heard. It's a shame I'm writing about firefighters and not bullies this time."

"But you know what I'm saying. You could … purge yourself of all that bad energy. All those memories. Put them to good use. And it could be a healing experience for you."

"Maybe you're right. I could take notes for another project somewhere down the line."

"Or you could start vomiting words up right now, when you get home. Get rid of it, as much as you can. You'll feel better when you have to see him."

I don't bother telling her she's right. She's heard it enough from me by now.

I'M FEELING SLIGHTLY more human by the time I get home, though trudging upstairs to my apartment is still a chore with half a hangover. It's only when I'm nearing the top that I think of Matt and decide tiptoeing is a fun way to walk.

Somehow—this doesn't come as a surprise—he's already outthought me and stacked roughly ten books in front of my door. Right. The brain science books he was telling me about. Now, I have to move the books out of the way just to get the door open and get into the apartment.

Part of me wants to turn around and kick his door, but that would only give him the satisfaction of knowing he's gotten to me. Which is what he wants.

Instead, I ever so gently push the stack out of the way until it's possible to get around them without knocking the whole tower over and alerting him to my presence. Only when I start moving them into the apartment do I see the sticky note he left on the top book.

Maybe this will help you get over the sting of being wrong. Again.

"Ooh, I just hate you." I crumple up the note and throw it at his door, for lack of anything else to do.

Chapter Eight

I NOW KNOW what it must feel like to sit down at a peace summit with a longtime foe looking back at you from the other side of the table with nothing in the world to do but figure out a way to coexist without any bombs going off.

Though, in my case, the bombs would be entirely mine. I'd be the one blowing things up.

While Bryce would be trying his best to make peace.

I can tell right away that making peace is all he wants to do.

"Thank you so much for coming." He's sporting a more rugged look than he was when we saw each other over the weekend. Wearing a turtleneck sweater and jeans that somehow make him look even better than the tux did. I would find this outfit painfully more appealing if it were on any other man in the world.

Heck, even if he were Matt. It's not like I'm immune to his hotness.

"Of course. My grandmother paid a pretty penny for my evening with you."

He smiles slightly. It's obvious he's still unsure of himself and unclear of what's going on with me, why we're together, how it came to be. "She's generous. I didn't know you had wealthy connections."

"How would you have ever gotten the chance to learn anything about me? You were busy tripping me, calling me names, pushing me around, laughing at me. And not just me, of course."

Wow, this isn't going well, is it? I know I'm supposed to play nice, but I'd rather pull out my own teeth.

Seeing him again has brought all those old issues to the surface. I've spent the past two days writing out everything I could remember and how it made me feel, how much I hated him back then, how much he made me hate myself. I was even feeling better for a while. I convinced myself to let bygones be bygones.

But now, with him in front me, all that has been wiped away.

He sighs, leaning back in his chair. It's a fairly casual restaurant—cute, sort of a hipster vibe. People feel free to relax here. Nobody cares very much that he looks upset. Except for me.

"I wish there were something I could say to take it all back. I really do. I swear, from the bottom of my heart, I've spent years trying to make up for the things I did back then. I know it sounds corny," he admits when I snicker, "but it's true. Back then, I didn't care who I hurt. I wanted somebody else to hurt the way I was hurting. That's all I wanted."

A tale as old as time.

"Lots of people hurt though. I went through a lot of hurt when my parents died. I didn't go around pushing people down the stairs."

"I know. It was wrong. I went through therapy. I also went to military school." He smirks at my gasp. "Yeah. And you know what? I needed it. Big time. It straightened me out."

"It looks that way—from your bio, I mean."

He nods, solemn. "I hated it at first, of course. I tried to break out. I was so full of myself. I hate the kid I was then, really. It took years, but one of the shrinks there finally got through to me. I'd … had some challenges when I was a kid. Things I don't like to talk about." He looks down at the table, his jaw twitching.

"I see."

"When I shared them with the shrink—once I trusted him enough to share—he helped me connect the dots. I had to process what had happened. I had to get through it. Once I did, things fell in line. Don't get me wrong." He chuckles. "It wasn't overnight. But I got my act together."

"I'm really glad you did." And I am.

I'm not a monster. I'm not some cold, unsympathetic beast. If what he's telling me is true—and it sounds like it is unless he's a heck of an actor—he was only lashing out as a kid. It was painful and terrible for me and everyone he bullied, but he was a child. It's easy to forget that part.

"Thanks. But that doesn't change what I did. Or how sorry I am." He leans in, arms on the table. "I really am sorry. I can tell you're still mad at me, and I don't blame you. I'd be mad too. I put you through some awful shit, didn't I?"

His choice of words makes me laugh. I can't help it.

"Yeah, you did. Awful. You made me dread going to school."

"Oh, Kitty." His face just about crumples up. "It kills me. It really does. Since I wasn't kidding when I said I had a crush on you back then."

Darn my treacherous cheeks for flushing. "Not really."

"Yes, really. Even though you were younger, even though there were cute girls my age. Of course, none of them would look at me. I was a prick; what can I say? They had better taste than that, even at the age of thirteen. But you stuck out to me."

"Why? How?"

He shrugs, which brings my focus to his thick, muscular shoulders. "You just did. You were pretty, and you had a lot of friends. You were always laughing with them. Teachers liked you. Even the maintenance people liked you. I guess that drew me in even though I told myself you were a nerd for it. But you caught my attention, and I didn't know what to do about it. I was too young and stupid and scared."

"I was sure you hated me, and I had no idea why."

"*I hated me.* Not you. I reached out to Toby Powers, the kid I sent down the stairs. I wanted to make things right." He grins, a little sad. "He told me to go fuck myself."

"Oh, I'm sorry."

"It's okay. I deserved that." He meets my gaze. "What about you? Do you think I should go fuck myself?"

Do I? I told myself earlier that he should, that I wanted him to do that and a whole lot worse.

But now? Now that I know where he was coming from and why he acted the way he did? "No, I don't think you should do that."

I'm the big softie Hayley made me out to be after all. I talk a good game, but I can't follow through when the time comes.

His sigh is long, deep. "Thank you." He even looks lighter, happier. The worry lines in his forehead and at the corners of his eyes smooth out.

"What I think you should do is help me write a book." I pull out my notepad and pen, placing them next to the silverware.

Our server hasn't come by yet, which is just as well. We had things to talk over.

We still do in fact.

"Yeah, what's that all about? I've been wondering ever since you mentioned it. And why did your grandmother pay for this?"

"Do you want the long story or the abridged version?"

"Abridged? You sound like a writer." He winks. "I want the full story. I'm not in any hurry."

Well, he asked for it. By the time I finish up, we're halfway through our burgers.

"So, here we are. I needed a firefighter to use for this next book. My grandmother knew where to find them and offered to put up the money. What was I supposed to do otherwise? Haunt the local firehouse until somebody agreed to go out with me?"

He snorts around a mouthful of fries. "It might've worked. Those long shifts get awfully boring sometimes, being around the same people you've been with for so many hours."

"You work long shifts?" *Oh good, I'm already getting information.*

But he frowns when he sees me starting to take notes. "Can we just talk right now? Besides, that's not anywhere near as interesting as the job gets. I'd be glad to give you a tour of the station whenever you want. You can meet more of the guys there, and they'll tell you just about anything you'd wanna know about what we do."

"That would be great. I'd really appreciate that."

"No problem. I'll text you my schedule, and you can let me know when you'll be coming by."

"Okay." Now, I feel silly for bringing out the notepad, so I have to say something. "I mean, I figured this would be the only time we got together, so I wanted to learn as much as I could."

He tilts his head to the side. "Is that what you want? I'd understand. This was only supposed to be a one-time thing. I shouldn't have assumed you'd want to see me again."

Is it what I want? Now that we're talking like two grown-ups, now that I see how he's turned his life around, do I want to see him again? It's an honest question.

Because no matter how many times I tell myself this is for a book and nothing more, there's part of me that knows better. Bryce has grown into a man with a sense of humor, a good attitude, a conscience—and a killer smile.

And that could prove dangerous.

The book is what matters though, which is why I nod. Isn't it? That's the only reason. "Sure, I want to see you again. To learn about the fire station and what you do for a living."

A smile flits across his face before he pops what's left of his burger into his mouth. "Fair enough."

Chapter Nine

"I HOPE YOU won't be disappointed." Bryce steps aside to usher me into the firehouse the afternoon after our date.

It's still weird, being near him. I make it a point to squeeze past without brushing against his flat torso or ridiculously broad chest. Call it old habits dying hard.

"Why would I be disappointed?"

There's a huge truck in the bay, all gleaming and shiny. It doesn't seem quite as massive as it did when I was a kid, but it's still overwhelming. "I remember coming here when I was little."

"That's right. I guess you would've lived near here back in the day."

"Less than half a mile away." It's not easy to put on a bright smile. Being in this neighborhood is like a punch to the gut.

I wish I could be happy here and wrap myself in warm memories and all that. But this is where my parents died. Where they were struck by a drunk driver down the street from our apartment.

A book is a book, and I have to write it. Which

means I have to take an opportunity where I see one.

I only wish I'd known before agreeing to stop in that Bryce worked out of this particular company.

"Well, for better or worse, I don't think much has changed around here in the last twenty years." He waves me on, walking ahead of me. "You'd have to ask one of the old-timers about that though."

"Hey, I heard that." A man with a mostly bald head fringed in gray sits behind a desk in an office we stop at on my little tour.

"Jim Henry, our captain." Bryce steps aside while I shake the captain's hand.

"Don't tell me you're involved with this piece of work." Jim nods toward Bryce.

"Oh, no!" All right, maybe that was a little too loud. Maybe I sounded a little too horrified. At least Bryce doesn't look terribly offended. "No, uh, I'm writing a book featuring a firefighter, and Bryce was nice enough to offer to show me around. For research. That's it." *Shut up, Kitty. That's enough.*

"A book about firefighters?" Jim chuckles, shaking his head. "Everybody thinks what we do is so exciting. You'd be disappointed to know the truth."

"Isn't that good though?" I look back and forth between the two of them. "The fewer fires you have to fight, the better, I would guess."

"Oh, for sure." Bryce nods. "But the rest of the time, we hang around, doing paperwork, maintaining the equipment, working out."

I can't help but grin. "Not the sort of stuff my readers want to read about, I don't think. But that's what fiction's all about. I'll make something up to hold their attention."

Jim laughs at this before going back to work.

"Our workout room." Bryce nods toward an open door, through which I can see a few weight machines and a couple of treadmills. "I'd call it a gym, but we'd have to update a few things for it to deserve that status."

"Do you work out here a lot?" *Wow.* I really need to start thinking about what my questions might sound like before I let them tumble out of my mouth. "I mean, as opposed to having a membership somewhere else."

If he finds this funny, he does a good job of hiding it. Leaning against a brick wall, he folds his thick arms, and it takes pretty much every ounce of my self-control to keep me from ogling his biceps. He's wearing a T-shirt snug enough to show off his considerable muscles.

"It doesn't make sense to have a membership anywhere else. My shifts here are usually twenty-four hours at a time, if not thirty-six."

"You sleep here, I assume?"

"No. I spend the entire thirty-six hours awake."

So, he feels comfortable enough to joke around a little. I guess that's a good thing, though it still doesn't seem right. Him calling the shots, deciding when we get to joke around and be friendly.

I'll let it go, for now.

"Ha-ha. So, what? It would be a waste of money to have a membership at a gym?"

"That was my point, yeah. I work out at home on the days I'm not here. You wanna see the bunk room? Where we sleep?" He winks before turning away, leading me farther down the hall.

After I look around in there—rows of cots really, not much more than that—we head into the kitchen.

"This is where we gather for the most part."

He introduces me to the seven firefighters sitting around a long table. Two are playing checkers, one's reading a book, and the other four are playing cards.

Another man is at the stove, stirring an enormous vat of spaghetti sauce.

"That smells delicious," I offer with a smile.

"You might feel a little different about it if you had to eat it for days." Bryce gestures to a freezer chest. "We usually cook a few things in bulk twice a month to feed us for a while."

"That makes sense. You never know when you'll have time to spend on it." I take a peek inside and find tons of food storage containers marked with dates and names of dishes.

It all feels sort of boring, but I would never say that out loud.

Besides, they all know how boring their job looks to outsiders. Jim already joked about that.

"Anything you wanna know?" Bryce looks around. "Questions? Thoughts?"

Nothing like being put on the spot. All seven heads swivel in my direction—eight, counting the guy at the stove.

"Um … yeah. What's it like, fighting fires?"

There's a moment of silence before everyone bursts out laughing. Not nastily, not rudely.

But still, nobody wants to be laughed at.

"Hey, hey, hey." Bryce holds up his hands and raises his voice to be heard over them. "It's a fair question. How would she know? Just because none of you are used to being around a beautiful woman—"

"Not true." One of the men holds up his left hand, where a gold ring shines.

"Yeah," another one calls out. "And I was at that auction too, don't forget."

Right, this is one of the other bachelors. I didn't recognize him at first.

"Oh!" The guy at the stove finally gets it. "Is this the girl who won you?"

The entire tone in the room changes. Now, they're the ones who want to ask me questions.

"Did you lose a bet?"

"What did you see in him?"

"You mean, this is his idea of a date?"

I have to answer that last one since it would sort of be an insult to both of us. To him, for thinking this is a date, and to me, for accepting this as a date after paying all that money for the pleasure of his company.

"This isn't a date. We already went out."

"And you wanted to see him again?"

This sets off another round of laughter.

Bryce takes it well. So, his good sense of humor isn't an act. "All right, okay. We can't all be as charming as you losers." He gives one of the men a playful punch on the shoulder, and they laugh together.

I wonder what these laughing, teasing men would think if they knew I once watched Bryce punch a smaller boy until he cried. That version of Bryce is as far away from the present version as we are from the moon. He's a different person now.

Hold up now. That's my voice of reason, a voice that sounds a lot like Hayley.

And the voice is right. I can't let myself think about him too much, and I definitely can't like him too much. It would feel like I was betraying my younger self.

Childish? Yes. But no less true.

The ear-splitting alarm makes me yelp in surprise. But I'm the only one since everyone's out of the room in a flash. Even the cook after he turns off the heat under the pot. I'm left trotting behind them as they hurry to the bay.

There's a fire somewhere.

I watch with my heart in my throat as the men put on their equipment with speed and efficiency like I've never seen before. Bryce is the one who gets most of my attention as he puts on his coat, his respirator, his helmet. I'm pretty sure he's already forgotten I was ever here, and I guess that's for the best. He needs to have his head in what he's about to do.

What must it be like for them to suit up for a fire and have no idea exactly what they're going to find when they arrive on the scene? Sure, they can get all the information possible before leaving and can get reports along the way.

But there's got to be something lost in translation. There can't be anything quite like arriving at the fire scene and seeing, feeling, battling it.

The truck's siren rings out through the bay as the men run for the truck. Bryce looks my way just once before climbing on, and I know we'll have to pick this up another time.

It isn't until the truck pulls away and I follow it, stopping on the sidewalk to watch it race down the street, that I find myself hoping for the chance to see him again. Soon.

Chapter Ten

"YOU'RE STILL THE asshole I went to school with." Nina turned her back on Larsen with a lump in her throat. A lump she hoped he hadn't heard come through in her voice. The last thing she wanted was for him to think of her as being weak.

She wasn't weak. She was strong, she was capable, she was miles away from the little girl she used to be.

"I've grown. You said so yourself."

"I meant, physically." She sighed, blowing a few strands of hair out of her eyes. "You grew physically."

"I'm a man now. I was a boy then."

He was so close. She could feel the heat from his body, even through her coat. Or was her mind playing tricks on her? Was she believing what her hormones told her was so?

"You're still an asshole."

"You don't know that. For all you know, I'm the man you watched interacting with the kids you teach. You liked me then, didn't you?"

"No," she lied.

"You're lying," he whispered with laughter in his voice. "You were smiling. It was genuine. Not forced."

"The kids didn't need to see how I really felt about

you written all over my face. Kids are very sharp. They know what's up."

Were they seriously talking about this?

They wouldn't be if he hadn't practically stalked her. Hanging out in front of the school, waiting for her to come out. He was lucky she hadn't called the cops on him. Hell, it might still be an option. If he pulled this again, she would.

"It's freezing out here."

Was that his hand on her shoulder? She shook it off like his touch burned.

"No kidding. I'd be halfway home by now if it wasn't for you being out here."

"Sorry. I'll let you go." He backed away, his boots crunching the gravel under them. "I only wanted to tell you how sorry I was."

"Yeah, you're sorry. That does a lot of good." She turned on her heel and walked away from him.

He didn't deserve another second of her time. Not another breath. Nothing. He was nothing.

She stalked out of the playground and continued down the street, fists thrust into her coat pockets in an attempt to keep her hands warm. Why had he shown up? Why had he shown himself to her at all? Wasn't seeing him again bad enough?

Wasn't it bad enough that he was charming and adorable with the kids? That they had obviously loved him?

Why did he get to have a good life after what he had done to her and the other kids in school? When he'd given her a freaking complex she still struggled against so many years later?

"Hey." The voice came from a truck on the street, rolling slowly to keep pace with her. "You didn't say you'd be walking. It's freezing out. Let me drive you home."

OKAY, SO MAYBE I'm drawing a little too much from real life. Sue me.

Maggie thinks it's okay. In fact, she thinks it's a great idea to add the bully element, though my hero is the furthest thing from a bully in his adult life. He's a firefighter who was just written up in the newspaper for saving a pair of toddlers from a house fire after their parents were unable to rescue them. Inspired by this, the heroine's boss thought of a nice idea for a field trip for the kids. A day at the firehouse, a chance to meet a hero.

Unfortunately, the hero firefighter happens to be her childhood bully. A bully who led to her being homeschooled until college.

They have their challenges, my hero and heroine.

They also need to get it on. Fast. And hard. Because that's the one thing Maggie keeps pushing for. Not realism. Not deeper emotion.

More sex. Sloppy, messy, graphic sex.

Maybe it's time to consider the hate sex she suggested. These two would be perfect for that. My heroine, whose name is currently Nina—unless I come up with something I like better—hates her bully but can't deny how hot he is. And, yes, he was great with her students when she brought them in for their little visit.

Which only made him more attractive.

And he's super attracted to her too. Not only that, but he also wants to make up for the past. He's eager to. Desperate to in a way since he wants her. But he'll have to break through her icy resolve in order to get what he wants.

Darn it.

I'm gonna have to ask for advice on this, aren't I?

Which is what takes me across the hall to Matt's front door. We haven't really spoken since the night of the auction, which makes it almost a week now. I don't know if he's still annoyed with me for putting him on the spot or if he's plotting my demise.

It could go either way.

But this is too important to let my squeamishness stop me.

"Oh, hello, stranger." Matt leans against his front door, wearing nothing but a pair of jeans. His hair is wet and looks like he just raked his fingers through it. "You caught me just out of the shower."

"Lucky me." Dang it, there are still moments when his hotness catches me off guard. "You must've had a busy morning if you're only getting out of the shower now."

"What, have you memorized my schedule?"

I hate that smirk. I hate it. I hate it. At least it helps me forget his hotness. I have that working in my favor anyway. "I know you work out in the morning because you've told me so. And it only makes sense that you'd take a shower after working out."

"Okay, okay. I forgot you're a detective. So, what's up? Are you here to thank me for lending you those books?"

I haven't touched them since I moved them into the apartment. "Uh, no. I need some guidance on a scene I have to write."

And that smile. That knowing smile. I could smack it off his face. "Does it have to do with silky petals?"

"No, I don't write like that anymore." I wish like mad that I'd never shown him the scene I was trying to write that first day, right after Maggie told me to heat things up or get used to never selling another book.

"But it has to do with sex."

"Yes, okay? Yes, it does." I fold my arms, lifting my brows. "So? So, you wanna know what the scene's about or what?"

"I know what it's about." He holds his hands at hip height, like he's grasping another pair of hips while thrusting his pelvis forward.

"You're disgusting."

"It's sex, Kitty."

"I don't need you to mime it for me, Matt."

He's laughing as he follows me across the hall to my apartment with Phoebe at his heels. I've sort of given up on the idea of keeping Phoebe out of my place. She likes me.

"Fine. What's got you stuck this time?"

I can only growl when he flops down on the couch, crossing his ankles on the coffee table while Phoebe sits beside him. "Make yourself at home."

"Hey. You're lucky I don't charge you a consulting fee for these little sessions of ours. I don't work for free."

"This isn't work."

"You know what I mean. I'm a busy guy. My time is valuable."

"Are you trying to get a free lunch out of me? Is that what you're trying to say?" I toss him my phone, the app already open. "Order something. Get me my tofu. Then, tell me what it's like to have sex with somebody you don't like."

"What?" He almost drops the phone, bursting out laughing the way I knew he would.

"You're so predictable." I sit at my desk instead of anywhere near him since I don't particularly enjoy being that close to him when he's laughing at me.

"I'm sorry for laughing. No, really," he insists when I roll my eyes. "You caught me off guard. Why would you assume I would know anything about that?"

"Don't you?"

"Hate sex? Not really." He looks up at the ceiling and blows out a slow sigh, like he's thinking it over.

"Not even sex with somebody you didn't like but thought was hot?"

"Oh, sure." He grins, turning his face toward me now. "Yeah, I know how that goes."

"How do you do that? How can you disconnect the physical from the emotional and mental?"

"You just do." He lifts a shoulder while scratching Phoebe behind the ears.

Sweet pup. I envy her sometimes. She doesn't have to think about things like this—or about anything at all. She gets her scratches and her treats and her walks, and that's all she cares about.

"I can't imagine that, and that's my problem." I have to rest my head on the desk. "My head hurts."

"You're overthinking it—the way you do all the time."

"Thanks so much. You're so nice to me."

"Okay …"

"Really, I'm so lucky to have you in my life."

"Why do you come to me for advice if this is how you're going to act when I give it to you?" He laughs. "You need to get your head out of it. That's my advice to you and to your characters. Because that's how it works. Letting your body do the thinking for you."

He shifts his position, now facing me. I can tell from the sparkle in his eyes that he's feeling mischievous. "I guess you've never been in a situation like that?"

"Like what?"

"A situation where you're so turned on, so hot for somebody, that nothing else matters? Like, you'll die if you can't rip their clothes off." He balls up one fist, pressing it against his stomach. "It's a burning in your core. It doesn't even make sense. It's too strong to resist."

Oh. Why is my mouth dry all of a sudden? And when was the last time I breathed?

"Um ... no. I've never been in a situation like that. When I hate you, I hate you. Nothing's going to change my mind. Not even a burning in my core."

"You haven't met the right man yet." There's that naughty smile. Like clockwork.

"I guess I haven't." Leaning back in my chair, I fold my arms. "You up to the challenge?"

He bites his lip. "Ooh. Spicy. I like this version of you."

"Thanks."

"Kitty's found her claws."

"Oh, gag me." But it makes me laugh, and he joins me. "Don't quit your day job."

"You're the writer." He looks me up and down. "Had your date yet?"

Dang. That's right. We still haven't talked about that.

"Yes, in fact. It was casual. Burgers. No big deal."

"And is he helping you write about firefighters?"

"He will. I have plenty of notes I took after he showed me around the firehouse."

"How nice of him."

He's being way too calm.

"What gives? What are you trying to get at? Why are you asking me these questions?"

"Because I saw you talking with the guy after the auction ended. Your body language wasn't exactly warm."

"How would you know?"

"Because you've given me the same cocked-hip, folded-arms, jutted-chin pose before. I think you gave it to me out in the hall." He looks down at the dog. "Didn't she? Yes, she did. She jutted that chin way out."

"It was all a big misunderstanding."

"Was it?" He looks at me, still petting the dog's head. "You sure?"

I hate him. I hate him so much.

"You talked to my grandmother, didn't you? I knew I should've looked for you afterward to make sure you weren't embarrassing me."

"You mean, the way you embarrassed me by putting me on the spot in front of that cougar? Because you did, and she is."

"Oh, I'm not arguing that. She totally is."

"Why did you do that to me?"

"I don't know. It seemed like a good idea at the time." When he doesn't look away, still staring at me with those penetrating eyes of his, I have to break down. "I'm sorry. That must've been uncomfortable."

"Not really." He stands, grinning, while I have to remind myself to not, under any circumstances, stare at his ridiculous torso. "I mean, I went for more money than anybody else there. No, it was definitely comfortable."

"Okay, okay. Get out of here. I need to get back to work."

"What about the food?"

"I'll leave it in front of your door. I mean it," I growl when he makes a face. "I have to get back to this."

"Remember, a burning in your core. You don't care about anything but how much you need to tear somebody else's clothes off."

"I'll keep that in mind." And I will.

But it's no help at all. Not when I've never felt that sort of all-consuming lust before in my entire life.

Chapter Eleven

"WHY AM I waiting for the other shoe to drop?"

Hayley's laughter rings out on the other end of the call. "You're always waiting for that, aren't you?"

"Nice. Thank you."

"Because you don't trust him yet; that's why." She pauses. "And because it seems a little strange, I guess. Asking you to meet him at Rockefeller Center."

"I mean, seriously. We've spent all of a couple hours together, tops, and he's asking me on a date to the rink."

"Are you going to ice skate?"

"Do I strike you as a masochist?" No way would that end well. I couldn't even handle roller skating as a little girl.

"Who knows? It could be sort of romantic. Letting him hold you up …"

"I'm not in this for romance, remember?"

"No. Just for a romance book."

She can't see me rolling my eyes, so I do it several times for good measure. "Whatever. You know what I mean. I've written enough books by now to be able to make things up when I have to. He's already given me plenty of inspiration."

"Really?" She pauses for effect. "Then, why did you accept his invitation to go out tonight?"

"You going to law school did me no favors."

"Case closed."

"Don't spike the ball, Hayley. You've already won. To answer your question, I don't know. I guess I wanted to check in with him after watching him leave on that call the other day. It was exciting and jarring and freaky. I mean, what do you think it must be like to leave on a call and not know how things are going to turn out?"

"Hmm. That must be hard, but it's gotta be the sort of thought they get used to and learn to ignore. You can't live your life in fear. You have to do your job. You have to live."

"I guess so. I wanted to ask him about that tonight, to get his thoughts on it."

"What a romantic date idea."

"It's not a date."

"Right. We'll see if you're still feeling that way when you get home."

It's actually a relief to get off the phone, which is rare when it comes to conversations with my best friend. Bryce has my nerves on edge, combined with Hayley's question about why I'm meeting up with him again tonight.

Why am I doing this? Because I have a hard time

turning people down. And it seemed important to him.

Which is why I get out of the car in front of the crowded center, where the famous Christmas tree was just lit last night. It's beautiful, as always, and people are elbowing each other out of the way to get pictures of it. Just like New Yorkers, ready to throw a punch for the sake of a good picture of a Christmas tree. The spirit of the season.

"Hey!" Bryce waves at me over the heads of the people between us.

He's in a turtleneck again. The man found what works for him and stuck with it; I'll give him credit for that much. He looks fantastic.

I truly wish I hadn't noticed that first and foremost. I truly wish I could disconnect my girlie feelings and my lady-parts feelings from my brain.

"Hi." I keep my hands in my pockets when we reach each other, just in case he wants to go in for a hug. The fewer chances for awkwardness, the better.

"I'm glad you came." Darn it, the flush on his cheeks due to the cold December air makes him handsomer than ever. "I was afraid you'd ditch me since you toured the firehouse."

I sure wanted to. "Actually, I'm glad to have the opportunity to see you again." *Yes, that's right. Keep it civil but distant. Professional.*

"Really?" His eyes light up.

"I was wondering what it's like to go out on a

call and not know how things are going to turn out. I was hoping you could tell me."

The light leaves his eyes, but he smiles a little just the same. "Right. There are still things you want to know."

"Was everybody okay?"

"Sure. You would've heard about it on the news if we weren't."

"Of course. I didn't think about that." Nor did I think about how rotten I'd feel when he expressed disappointment. But, I don't owe him anything. I don't have to like him.

He looks toward the skating rink. "Take a spin with me. My treat. And we can talk about things while we skate."

"No, no, no." I laugh, waving my hands. "No, I don't skate. Believe me, it's for the best."

"Come on." He flashes a flirty smile. "I'm an excellent skater. I wouldn't let you fall."

"I honestly don't think it's a good idea. I'm so clumsy. I have no coordination."

"You're too hard on yourself. Come on." He inches away from me, toward the rink. "Come on, come on. There's still so much material I could give you for your book …"

"Hey, no fair! You don't get to hold that over my head."

"But it'll be so rich with details and true-to-life experiences …" He shrugs, still inching away.

Darn him.

"I swear, if you let me go and I break my ankle or something, I'll never forgive you. And I'll kill you off in my book."

It's against my better judgment, doing this, but now, I get the feeling it's an honor thing. Like, if I refuse, I'll look like a chicken.

And, yes, I know how immature that is. But I've never pretended to be mature.

Before long, we're both wearing skates, and I'm cursing myself for not being strong enough to say no.

"Come on. You can do it." He puts an arm around my waist and helps me onto the ice.

I'm too scared of what's about to happen to care that he's touching me.

"So, maybe you weren't too hard on yourself." He laughs when I almost fall over, holding me close to him. "You're not very good at this."

"No kidding! That's what I was trying to tell you!" I almost fall over again, but his arms have me locked in place. I can't go far without him reeling me back in.

"Try telling yourself you can do it. Stop thinking about how clumsy you are. Have you ever even tried to do this before?"

"No," I declare. Gosh, my heart is pounding so hard that I can barely stand it. I can barely even breathe.

And I hate to say it, but Bryce's nearness isn't helping much. He makes me feel slightly more secure, but there are all sorts of ways to be in danger.

"I didn't think so. Take a deep breath. I've got you. All you have to do is relax and let me move us around for a while. Keep you even and straight."

"I hate this," I admit with a laugh while kids half my age zip past us like it's nothing. I want to ask them if they've ever written a best-selling book. I bet they wouldn't be able to do that.

"Relax. Breathe. Stop psyching yourself out." He's holding me firmly against his body with our hands clasped as if we're waltzing. "You'll be able to skate circles around some of these people in no time."

We reach one end of the rink, and Bryce expertly turns us in a single, smooth motion.

When the heck did he find the time to learn to skate so well while serving in the military and fighting fires? Talk about a Renaissance man.

By the time we cross the ice again, I can breathe without feeling like I'm about to hyperventilate. "Okay, this isn't so bad."

"I thought you'd come around." He pushes off a little harder with one skate, making us pick up speed.

"Not that fast!" I find myself clinging to him, which throws us off-balance and sends us sprawling.

Funny, the number of things that can go through a person's head when they're in free fall. It doesn't take long to fall. A second, if that.

It might as well be a million years.

"Ow, ow, ow." Bryce disentangles himself from me. "That sucked."

"I'm sorry." It's amazing that the ice is still solid and cold, considering that my entire body is burning with shame and should be melting it by now. "I'm so sorry. Did I hurt you?"

"No, no. Just my ass, but that's no big deal." He works his way to his feet and then helps me to mine. I somehow manage to find my balance and not bring us both crashing down again. "I shouldn't have gone so fast."

"I warned you, I'm not coordinated."

"No, that's not it." He catches me around the waist and holds me in place. There's something alarming about his strength, about how steady and secure he seems even though we're both balancing on single blades. "You don't believe in yourself. You don't trust yourself."

Part of me wants to tell him he doesn't know the first thing about me and is in no position to give advice. I didn't ask for it. I don't even want it.

The other part of me—a much larger part, in all honesty—wants to trust it's nothing more than my belief in myself, or lack thereof.

And I want to believe he's looking into my eyes with genuine tenderness. That it would be okay to let him kiss me, that I wouldn't be leading myself into a whole lot of heartbreak if I gave in and let the moment take us where it wanted us to be.

"Will you do something for me?" A tender smile plays over his lips. "Will you come to the firehouse tomorrow night? We're having a Christmas party for kids in the neighborhood and giving out gifts and stuff. It's a lot of fun, seriously. I think you'd like it."

It's a sweet invitation. Still, I can't help but ask, "Why do you think I would have fun?"

"Because you used to love the holidays so much. You decorated the front of your locker and everything."

Holy cow. I completely forgot about that. "You remember that?"

"Of course. And you're wearing earrings in the shape of Christmas trees."

"Fair enough."

"And while you're still wearing your coat, the sweater underneath has reindeers stitched into it. I noticed when we both went ass over teakettle a few minutes ago."

"I just bought it and figured it would keep me warm tonight."

His smile widens until it's practically blinding. "You still love the holidays. And I promise, when you see how much fun the kids have, you'll be glad you came. And you'll also have another chance to get to know the others, including the ones who were off earlier this week."

"Hmm. That's true."

"And I'll get to see you again." His arms tighten ever so slightly around my waist. "I can't pretend to be completely generous. I'll be getting something out of it too."

He's too tempting. Too tall, too strong, too gorgeous, too hot. Too everything.

Just enough of everything to keep me from pulling away when Bryce lowers his head and places a soft, gentle kiss on my upturned mouth.

Chapter Twelve

"SO, WHAT HAPPENED?"

"That was it." I look at Hayley over the display of neatly folded clothing between us. "Should there have been more than that?"

"You know what I mean." She sighs, going through a stack of sweaters, searching for the right size. "What happened after that? He kissed you. And then what?"

"Not much more could happen before we got off the ice, I'll tell you that much. Not if we didn't want to break our necks."

"I told you skating would be romantic."

"It wasn't romantic. It was terrifying."

"Both lead to a surge of adrenaline, don't they? Romance and terror?" She does a little happy dance on finding the size she was looking for and then holds the sweater up for inspection. "What do you think? For my sister."

"It's gorgeous. She'll love it." I'm barely paying attention, which probably makes me a really bad friend. It's just that I can't stop thinking about what it meant to be kissed by Bryce. And about how, now that I'm being honest with myself, the sight of him leaving to fight that fire gave me a feeling of uneasiness in the pit of my stomach and a lot of anxiety.

Hayley looks at me as she slides the sweater into the basket she's carrying over one arm. "Haven't found anything yet?"

I have to snicker at this. "The only people I have to shop for are you, my grandmother, Maggie, and Lois. The latter two get gift baskets every year since what other option do I have? I can't imagine buying anything else for them. Grandmother?" I look around at the inside of the store. "I doubt she'd want anything they offer here. It's a little young for her. And a little too not fancy."

"I'm sure she'd be glad to get whatever you gave her."

"Oh? So, I should go with something like this?" I hold up a faux fur jacket, dyed a festive shade of green.

"Okay, maybe not that."

"And I can't shop for you right in front of you," I finish with a shrug.

"So, why'd you come out? I know you hate shopping in actual stores."

I follow her to a rack of dresses and watch as she flips through them. For one thing, observing her as she shops gives me an idea of what to get for her. Every so often, she'll come across something and smile a little or tap her chin like she's thinking of buying it for herself—before remembering she's supposed to be shopping for her family.

"Is it enough to say, I'd put up with all kinds of torture just to spend time with you?"

That earns me a tremendous eye roll. "Oh, sure, I believe that one."

"It's sort of true. Hey, I was gonna go to that office Halloween party with you. Remember? That would've been a tremendous sacrifice."

"If you'd gone."

"I was going to! You decided we weren't going when you found out who was performing there."

Granted, it's a shame I didn't get to see Dustin fall off the yacht—after how he hurt my feelings, he deserved it—but I got plenty of enjoyment from watching video taken by Hayley's coworkers.

She's smiling when she looks back over her shoulder. "And you wanted to dish about what happened last night too. Don't pretend."

"You wanted the details. Don't act like I hunted you down and put a gun to your head, demanding to tell you every little thing."

"Okay, fine." She goes back to looking through the racks. "Anyway, I'd assumed things would go a lot worse than they did last night. What with the chip you have on your shoulder about Bryce and all."

"I wouldn't call it a chip." I sniff, a little offended.

"Sorry." She glances at me. "A boulder."

"Hush. Spoken like a girl who was never bullied."

"You're right. I got lucky, I guess."

"You were always cool." I hold up an adorable dress, soft pink, printed with polka dots. "What about this?"

"That's something you'd like. Not my sister."

"Hmm. Wouldn't it be nice if somebody were to buy this for me in a size four?" I shrug while replacing the dress.

"Wouldn't that be nice?" She barely hides a laugh as she moves to the next rack.

How she can shop so casually while what feels like hundreds of people are crammed together all at once, fighting for the last pair of leggings, is a mystery. She walks around in a bubble, this girl. A charmed bubble.

"I'm just saying ..." I look back at the dress, which is super cute and would look great on me. Granted, I'd have to find someplace to wear it once the weather warms up. It's a little dressy for my roof. "You might wanna pick that dress up before it's gone."

"What if I already bought you something?" Before I can retort, she changes the subject. "So, he kissed you. Was it any good?"

"He didn't stick his tongue down my throat in the middle of the rink, if that's what you're asking. He has a little decency."

"What a shame," she sighs.

"I was on blades. I don't know if I could've stayed upright if he had done any more than he did, so …"

"Did you feel tingly? Did you feel anything at all?"

"Besides surprised?"

"Besides surprised."

"I mean, yeah. It was nice. It was really nice. More than nice. I wanted him too."

"That's a good sign." She meets my gaze. "What next? Do you want there to be more?"

"I wish I could say. He's a great guy. He's good company. He's hot." I shrug. "But, you know, I don't feel a spark."

"You won't let yourself feel a spark. I think that's the problem."

"You're so wise, you know?"

"I know what I'm talking about, so don't get snippy with me."

"Have you ever considered writing an advice column? If the whole law thing doesn't work out?"

She's been friends with me long enough to know how to selectively ignore me. "You don't want to like him. Which is why you won't allow a spark." When I roll my eyes, she adds, "Kitty, you knocked him on his ass in the middle of the rink, all because he went too fast for you and you freaked out."

"That wasn't my fault!"

"My point is, he wanted to kiss you anyway.

That means something."

"It was his big idea for me to be on skates. I warned him."

"I hear you. But you're missing my point. He likes you, Kitty. He used to like you, and he likes you now. He's not the person he used to be. Why not let things happen the way they want to happen?"

"Oh, you know me. I think too much. I can't let myself be in the moment and enjoy things." And I certainly wish Matt's advice wouldn't come to mind at times like this.

"That's a true story." She grabs a pretty scarf and hat with a satisfied smile. "I think I'm finished with the family. I still have to pick up something for my Secret Santa at work. That's always awkward."

"I can't imagine." And I really can't since I've never worked in an office and therefore never been subjected to buying a gift for somebody I don't really know. "Alcohol?"

"No, because there might be people in the office who can't or won't drink." She shrugs. "It's a rule. So, maybe a gift card? But I don't want to look like I didn't put any thought into it. I'll be that girl who couldn't be bothered. I don't want that reputation."

"It could be worse. You could give them a candle that's been sitting in your closet for years."

"Damn it. I was just gonna suggest that."

"So, do you think I should go to that Christmas party today at the firehouse?"

"Don't even ask me, Kitty."

"Ask you what?" *Did I sound surprised enough? Do I look surprised enough?*

"Ask me to go with you. The answer is no."

"I wasn't going to!"

"You were." We inch our way up in line, behind at least eight other people waiting to be checked out. "God, this is when I remember why I hate shopping."

I should let it go, right? Yes, I should let it go. If I keep arguing the point, it'll look like I care too much. Like she caught me. Which she did. But she doesn't need to know.

"I wasn't going to."

"Fine, fine. Anyway, even if I wanted to go, I can't. I have too much work to do this weekend."

"Would you come with if you didn't have to work?"

"No, I probably wouldn't. It's not my scene, and Bryce isn't the firefighter I'm dating." She shrugs. "Sorry. You've gotta be a big girl. You're the one who said you'd go. You've gotta face the music."

Why am I low-key dreading this? I have no idea.

Bryce is a great person. Patient and gentle. The exact opposite of who I remembered him as. Maybe it's the sense of confusion. Not knowing what to expect. I haven't yet let go of my memories.

I need to do that.

"How's the book coming along?" We're finally at the front of the line, where Hayley dumps her items on the counter.

"It's coming along." I shrug. "A little slow, but they usually start slow."

The cashier looks back and forth between us. "You're a writer?"

"I am." I wave a hand while my cheeks flush. And it's not from the excessive heat in this over-crowded store.

"What do you write?"

"She writes romance." Hayley's grinning from ear to ear.

I'd like to say she's genuinely being a good friend right now, proud and all that. That she's not putting me on the spot the way I put Matt on the spot during the auction.

I only wish I could believe that.

"I love romance! Oh gosh, it's the only thing I read! What's your name?"

We're attracting attention now from the other girls behind the registers. "Um … you've probably never read me. Kitty Valentine."

"Kitty Valentine?"

I'm pretty sure dogs around the corner heard her since she was so high-pitched that my ears almost couldn't pick up her voice.

She puts a hand to her chest, bending over a little. "You're Kitty Valentine?"

"She is." Hayley puts an arm around my shoulders. "You're a fan?"

"A fan? Oh, yeah, you could say that." The girl—the tag on her shirt says her name is Meg—

waves her hands in front of her face like she's fighting back tears.

"Oh my gosh!" I honestly don't know how to navigate this. I've never met a fan like this before, in the middle of a shopping trip. "That's so sweet. I wish I knew what to say."

"Your more recent work is so hot," she whispers with a giggle. "I love it. Keep them coming, okay?"

"She's working on a new book right now." Hayley is enjoying this way too much. She knows too well how I clam up whenever I'm the center of attention.

"Did Matt put you up to this?" I mutter from the corner of my mouth while leaning over the counter for a selfie with Meg.

"I can't believe I'm meeting my favorite author!" Meg gushes. "And I wasn't even going to come to work today!"

It's hard to keep from smiling as we leave the store.

"See?" Hayley whispers. "Your work means something to people. It's easy to lose sight of that when you're busy trying to figure out your personal life and how it ties into your characters."

"You're right. It is. It's very easy to forget fans." And that little interaction was just what I needed to get in writing mode again.

My public wants to read what I have to say.

I should've recorded that meeting for Maggie's benefit. And for Lois's when it comes time to negotiate my new contract.

Chapter Thirteen

"WOW. YOU GUYS went all out!" I can't help but stand back and gape at the way the firehouse kitchen has been decorated.

Four days ago, it was just a kitchen. Not so much as a hint of decoration to be seen. A handful of firefighters sat around, killing time.

Now? There are at least six trees, fully decorated and dripping with tinsel. Red, green, gold, and silver garland is draped over just about everything. Potted poinsettias fill the corners and surround the trees and decorate the tables now set up to accommodate the kids and their families. There's music playing, tons of food, and roughly forty kids running between the bay and the kitchen, just about jumping out of their skin with excitement.

Which I'm sure is only helped by the cookies and cakes and candy canes they're eating like there's no tomorrow.

One of the firefighters hears me and shrugs with a sheepish grin. "We like to do it. And it makes the kids happy."

"It's terrific. And so sweet of you."

"Which one's yours?" he asks, surveying the kids.

"Oh, no, I'm not a mom or a nanny or anything like that. Bryce invited me." I look around. "Where is he?"

"He'll be out soon." The guy winks at me. "You'll see."

I'll see? Pretty cryptic, but I'll go along with it for now.

It's worth seeing the kids so happy. I can understand why it means a lot to the firefighters to put on a nice party for them.

Jim, the captain I met on Tuesday, can't hide a wide smile when he enters the kitchen. Several of the kids run to him, grabbing him around the legs—clearly, he is a favorite of theirs. It's really neat, seeing how much good the fire company does in the community.

Recognition washes over his craggy face as he joins me by the cookie tray. "I wondered if we'd see you again. I thought maybe we'd scared you away the other day."

"Not at all. It was a thrill to watch you all get ready to go out and fight a fire. Invaluable too. For research." *Gee, I sound like a super-fun person right now, don't I?*

He doesn't seem to mind, reaching past me to snag a cookie. "Don't miss out on the chocolate chips. They are murder on my waistline, but they taste like heaven."

"I've already had three," I confess with a giggle.

"They're my wife's 'signature recipe.' " He adds air quotes to this with a grin. "She only makes them during the holidays."

"She could sell them and make a mint." I nod toward the kids, who are all dancing to the upbeat music. "I'm sure their parents will thank you later for the sugar crash."

The adults are lingering around the station, chatting, sitting at the tables set up just for today.

"Hey, this is the time of year for sugar crashes." He folds his arms over his chest, laughing at the kids. "My wife and I, we never had any of our own. It's nice to see happy kids at this time of year."

He turns to me, looking me up and down. "So, what do you think about Bryce? He's a good one."

I have to laugh, a little sheepish. "I have to admit, I knew him back when we were kids, and he wasn't my favorite person. But time has changed him."

"Time changes all of us," he acknowledges with a nod. "Maybe you can convince him not to take so many risks when he's out on a call. None of us have been able to, I can tell you that much."

Just like that, all the hectic, high-energy excitement around me fades into the background as I focus in on what he just said. "What do you mean?"

"I guess he never told you about that." He shakes his head. "I wouldn't expect him to. He doesn't like to talk about the things he does."

"I don't understand."

Now, he looks uncomfortable. Like he wishes he hadn't said anything at all. "It's just that I've known a lot of guys like him. They're eager to be a hero. There's nothing wrong with wanting to help people but not if it means unnecessary risks. My job is to keep all of us safe."

"Are you saying he takes risks he shouldn't?"

Rather than answering right away, he motions for me to follow him. Along one wall of the kitchen is an array of plaques and pictures. Some of the pictures are decades old, sepia-toned, of men who fought fires long before I was born.

Others are more recent. I recognize Bryce in one of them. He's dressed well, shaking hands with the mayor, Jim and another uniformed man standing behind them.

"That's when he got his citation." Jim taps on the glass covering the picture. "That was a good day. I was proud of him; we all were."

Then, he turns to me, lowering his voice. "But he took an awful risk. Yeah, he saved those kids' lives, and that was a tremendous thing. But he almost died."

I suddenly feel cold inside, though the room is plenty warm, thanks to all the crazy, energetic bodies running around. "How? What happened?"

"He took off his respirator after I pulled him back. It was a house fire, burning out of control. A big house, one of those old, historic townhouses. So

JILLIAN DODD

much wood inside, so many flammable materials.

"He'd pulled out the parents along with a couple of the others, and I'd wanted him to sit back and catch his breath. He was already overwhelmed by the smoke and heat. But then somebody saw the kids waving from the third floor. The parents were unconscious, as the smoke had already gotten to them. We hadn't known until then that there were kids inside the house.

"What did Bryce do? Didn't even put his respirator back on, just took off running. I tried to stop him, but it was too late. He was already inside the house. I don't know exactly how he pulled it off, but he got them out of there.

"And then he spent a few days in the hospital. He could've easily gotten himself and those kids killed because he hadn't even taken the time to put his respirator on."

He sighs, shaking his head. "Don't get me wrong. Everybody wants to be a hero at some point. We all think we're going to have our moment, you know what I mean? But it would've taken him all of fifteen seconds to make sure he'd taken precautions before going in there—and even then, I wouldn't have sent him in alone.

"That's how he always has to do it. On his own, the way he wants to, and that's what worries me."

I'm not sure what to say. Bryce and I aren't that close yet, and it's not like anything I might say to him would make a difference. I'm sure he wouldn't like it if he knew Jim was talking about him this way behind his back. If anything, I can imagine the two of them have already had this out.

And I can imagine Bryce not wanting to listen to his captain's advice.

"I'll try to talk to him about it," I offer as gently as I can. "I can see why you're concerned about him."

"I've been with this company for thirty years. My dad was a firefighter. Two of my uncles were firefighters. Their father was too. Over the course of my life, I've seen what happens to people who want to be heroes. There's a time for that, and there's a time for listening and working as part of a team." He puts a hand on my shoulder, looking me straight in the eye. "Bryce is a good man. I would hate to see the world lose him."

I don't know what to say, but the shrieking of a few dozen kids pulls my focus away.

And all because Santa Claus has just stepped into the kitchen with a big bag slung over his shoulder. And now, something tells me I know exactly who's in that suit.

"Ho, ho, ho!" Bryce calls out in a booming voice as the kids swarm him. "Merry Christmas! What do we have here? A bunch of good boys and girls who deserve presents, I think!"

Meanwhile, parents are recording him on their phones and encouraging the one or two shy kids to say hello. They'd rather hide behind a chair or their mom's legs, unsure whether they can trust this red-suited guy.

Hayley would be so pleased. I've finally found my sexy Santa.

He takes a seat between two of the trees and calls the kids over one by one while the music goes on, and there's more eating and drinking and dancing.

"This is so great," one of the moms gushes as she fixes herself a plate of goodies. "The kids look forward to it every year."

"I think the guys who work here look forward to it just as much as the kids do," I venture since every one of them is wearing an almost-identical smile.

There's something magical about it, watching adults have just as much fun as kids, seeing their eyes shine.

"They do. We're so lucky to have them in the community." She looks me up and down, and I do the same to her in a vague sort of way. She's around my age, maybe a little older. "Do you live around here? I don't think we've met."

"I used to live in the area." I hold a hand to the side of my mouth, whispering, "Santa invited me."

"Oh, he did?" She chuckles, looking over to where Bryce is currently entertaining a pair of twin girls, one on either knee. Their mom is begging them to smile for a picture, but neither of them looks particularly thrilled.

"Do you know him?"

"Everybody knows Bryce. He's a familiar face around the neighborhood. Plays ball with the kids, mentors them, always smiling and positive." She then sighs softly, drawing her bottom lip under her teeth. "And he's not bad to look at, is he?"

"When he's not wearing a red suit with a pillow underneath? No, he's not bad to look at."

Indeed, now that I'm paying attention, it's clear several of the moms in the room wouldn't mind sitting on Santa's lap themselves. A pair of them murmur to each other, glancing his way, while a few just straight-up ogle him and laugh too loud when he makes a joke.

And why not? He's a dream. He's perfect. Everything I've heard about him makes me like him even more.

Except for the part where he takes too many risks. Maybe that is something worth talking about—and not only because I'm still researching for my book.

Why would he do that? Why does he feel like he always has to push himself so hard?

"I think that's everybody!" Bryce booms out in a voice much deeper than his own. "So many good boys and girls."

He then finds me, standing on the other side of the room. "I wonder if any of the grown-ups around here have Christmas wishes they want to share with Santa."

I point to myself, and he nods. The kids, meanwhile, are too busy playing with their new toys—dolls, trucks, stuffed animals—to care very much about what Santa does now. Who can blame them? They have what they came for, and now, they get to enjoy their gifts.

I wander over to him, shrugging. "I don't know, Santa. I think I might be a little too old for you to bring me any presents."

"Nonsense! All good girls and boys deserve presents at Christmastime." He pats his leg. "Come on. Tell Santa what you want for Christmas."

"Santa," I whisper once I'm close enough, "are you sure none of the other grown-ups around here will get jealous?"

He gives me a genuine laugh. "That's their problem. Come on. Tell Santa what he can bring you." He pats his leg again, and even a fake white beard can't hide his grin. He's loving this.

"Okay, okay." I perch on his lap and hope none of the other women in the room hate me too much. "Um, I'd like a best seller. A nice, new contract with my publisher. Hmm …"

"What about ice skates? Would you like a pair of ice skates?"

"No!" It wouldn't be right to give Santa a smack in front of a bunch of kids, which is what stops me from doing just that. "But I'd take coordination, if you're giving that out this year."

"Sorry, all out of that." He leans in a little closer.

KITTY VALENTINE DATES A FIREMAN

"How about you come to my place after this? We'll pack up some leftover food and talk some more about what you want this year."

Hmm. I have to admit, seeing him with the kids and hearing about what a positive influence he is on them makes me better inclined to accept. There's something unbelievably sexy about a man who's great with kids.

"That sounds like a good idea."

I mean, it is. Right? It's a good idea.

Just like taking a selfie and sending it to Hayley is a good idea.

Found my Santa without you.

Chapter Fourteen

"WELL, WELL, WELL ..." I have to stop in my tracks and take a look around the apartment once we're inside. "This is impressive. Just as impressive as your plan to get me here."

Bryce very actively avoids my gaze as he continues into the kitchen, leaving the bag full of food he packed up to bring with us. The kids weren't exactly interested in eating actual food. The lasagna, baked chicken, garlic bread, and cold salads didn't move very much. Not enough sugar in them.

"Did you hear what I said?" I admire the exposed brick walls, the original flooring.

This used to be a factory before it was renovated into apartments. Wooden beams dot the large, open living room. *How many people worked here? How many people touched these beams over the decades?*

"Hmm? Not really." He pokes his head out from the kitchen. "What'd you say?"

"Liar. You heard me. This was your plan all along." I slide out of my coat and shoot him a knowing look. "You knew that when I saw you with all those kids and how happy they were to see you and how terrific you were with them, I'd get all mushy inside and find you even more attractive than I did before."

"You find me attractive?" He leans against the wall, arms folded, a smirk slowly spreading.

"Right. Make sure that's the only thing you pay attention to." When he doesn't do anything but smirk even more than before, I add, "Yes, okay? I find you attractive. Along with every other woman in that firehouse today."

"Oh, them?" He waves a hand, looking away like he's embarrassed.

"Ahh, you don't like it when I turn the tables, do you?"

"Not so much, no."

"So, it bothers you that every woman at the party, married or otherwise, thought you were the tastiest thing to come their way since the invention of the cronut?"

"I think you're exaggerating." He still looks and sounds embarrassed as he hangs our coats in the closet. "It's not that big of a deal. They're nice women. The entire neighborhood is nice. Good people."

"I agree. I remember the sense of community there. That's one thing I'm missing now—community."

He waves me into the kitchen, which was clearly updated in the last few years. Shiny appliances, a dual oven, one of those fridges with the clear doors that I've always thought was so neat but I know I could never have for myself. Not with the normal condition of my refrigerator. Maybe it would encourage me to keep things neater in there.

"There's no community where you live? Rich people don't talk to each other?" He pulls out a couple of bottled waters. "Do you want anything else? Beer, wine?"

"No, this is fine. And I'm not rich. I'm far from rich. Though, yes, I guess rich people do live around there. There isn't that whole, you know ... *sitting out on the front stoop energy.*"

"Sure"—his smile widens—"I get what you mean."

"I only know one of my neighbors. The guy who lives across the hall. But I'm sort of an introvert, too, so that shouldn't come as a surprise. And I'm almost always working."

"A guy who lives across the hall, huh?"

"Don't even start. He's a friend—when I don't feel like killing him. Come to think of it, you might've met him at the auction! He was the last-minute addition, the only one who wasn't a firefighter."

"Oh, him?" His eyes widen while his lips pull back in a grimace. "So, that's who I'm competing against?"

I lean against the counter, looking him up and down. The thing is, he sounds like he means it. And I can't help but wonder whether I want him to mean it or not.

Here he is, standing in front of me. A tower of muscle, tan and healthy and droolworthy. He's got a face to match and a heart that seems like it was made from pure gold—that is, if the things I've heard about him so far are true, and I can't imagine why anybody would lie. I doubt he goes around, paying a personal PR team to spread good things about him.

I'd be the world's biggest idiot if I turned him down because of what had happened when we were kids. Not when the sight of him smiling in that playful way he's doing right now just about melts my panties.

"I didn't know you were competing against anybody." I shrug. "Though, I guess, if you were competing, he'd be tough competition. On paper, he's the perfect man."

"Really?" He lifts an eyebrow. "How?"

"Oh, I don't know. He's good-looking. He has a steady job that pays very well. He lives in a nice apartment in a great part of town. Who wouldn't jump at the chance to be with him?"

He offers a crooked grin. "Have you jumped?"

"God, no." I can't keep up the pretense. "The thought of the two of us together makes me cringe. We'd be like … mashed potatoes on top of chocolate cake."

"Which one of you is the cake?" He takes a step toward me and then another.

"Me, obviously. Devil's food." Yes, I'm flirting with him. Shamelessly in fact. But I'm a woman and he's a man and we're alone together and, darn it, I'm not made of stone.

He places his hands on the counter at my back, one on either side of me. "I believe that much. I believe that one taste of you could ruin a man for every other kind of cake in existence."

Now that he's near, I'm just about overwhelmed by the musky scent of his cologne, the heat coming from his body. My resistance is wearing thinner with every breath mingling between us. I close my eyes and nuzzle his neck.

"Look at me, Kitty." He waits for me to lift my eyes, to look into his. So dark, so warm. "Having you walk back into my life has been a gift. A miracle I didn't even know I wanted until it was right in front of me. And, yeah, maybe I invited you today so you could see how much fun the kids had and how everybody there likes me and gets along. So you could get an idea of who I am now. Not just what I tell you, but what other people have to say. I can't help it." He draws nearer until our bodies are practically flush. "I want you to like me."

"I do like you." His eyes are pulling me down, deeper and deeper, and I'm helpless. "I really do."

He catches my mouth with his before I can say anything else. Not that there's anything else to say. Not that I don't light up inside like a firefly the second our lips touch.

This isn't a kiss like last night either. Not a chaste little peck on the lips. No, this is much more. Deeper. Hotter.

He sinks his hands into my hair as my arms slide around his waist. This is nice. This is good.

It's even better when the kiss deepens, and my heart pounds faster than ever. He takes his time, moving slowly, tasting me. Nibbling my lips until my nerves sizzle and I want to throw him to the floor. Or for him to throw me. Either way, I'm not feeling particularly choosy right now, not with my body on fire.

Though even now, I'm aware of the pun. *Fire. Firefighter. Ha-ha-ha.* I need to get out of my head and into this. Because I want this. I really, really do.

His hands loosen and fall to my shoulders. He pulls back. "What's wrong? You went somewhere else."

"I didn't. Nothing's wrong." I try to force a smile, but it's weak. Shaky. I can feel it. I can see it in his eyes, too, when his brows draw low over them.

"Are you sure about that? Is there something wrong? Did I move too fast?"

"Gosh, no." I hold his face in my hands. There's already a faint bit of stubble on his cheeks. "No, you're doing just fine. I have to get out of my head. I've always had a problem with that. It's dumb."

"It's not dumb."

"I just made a pun to myself, in my head, about

my body being on fire and you being a firefighter, but you're only making it worse instead of putting it out. I mean, that's pretty lame."

He winces. "Okay, a little lame. But not deadly lame."

"Thanks."

He kisses my forehead before resting his chin on top of my head. "You're a writer. Your brain is always going."

"It is. I wish I could turn it off. You have no idea of the torture."

Laughter rumbles in his chest. My hands rest there, on top of firm muscle. Under that muscle is a beating heart. A good heart. This is a good man.

A good man who stiffens a little, whose breath comes up short. "I never thought of that before."

"Of what?"

He pulls back, looking down at me. "Do you write about … everything that happens? Like … everything?"

Oh. This. I didn't think of this. Why didn't I think of this? "No, no, no. No, you don't have to worry about that."

"Because, you know, that could have an effect on a guy. Talk about being in your head."

I know I shouldn't laugh, but I can't help myself. At least I manage to keep it light and gentle. "No, all those scenes are up here." I tap my temple. "That's it."

His tension eases. "Okay. Because, you know,

that's a lot of pressure." He leans in again, hands on the counter, and gives me a slow smile. "Now, all we have to do is get you out of your head."

Which, of course, is exactly when my phone rings.

Bryce laughs softly, hanging his head while I roll my eyes and curse my luck.

"Maybe they'll give up," I suggest.

"They'd better."

But they don't.

"Sorry, sorry. I feel like I should get it. Nobody ever calls me, so it might be important." *Does that sound like a pitiful excuse? Probably. Though it's the truth too.*

I don't recognize the number, so I answer with trepidation, "Hello?"

"Kathryn? Kitty Valentine?" The voice is male. An older man. I feel like I should know it.

Especially since he called me Kathryn. That's what finally brings everything together.

"Peter? Is that you?" And now, my heart is in my throat, and I can barely breathe. "What's the matter?"

He draws in a deep, shaky breath. "It seems your grandmother is ill. I'm at the hospital with her."

Chapter Fifteen

I KNEW THIS was going to happen someday. I just didn't want it to be today or this year or this decade.

I run from the car. Throw myself through the revolving door into the emergency room. Ask where I can find my grandmother.

The girl at the desk tells me she's been moved to the ICU and then directs me to the elevator. I can barely stand still as I wait to reach her floor, bouncing on the balls of my feet with my heart racing and my stomach in knots. I'm so glad we never took the time to eat at Bryce's since I would've lost it all by now. Probably at the moment Peter told me he found my grandmother on her bedroom floor.

The nurse who greets me when I get off the elevator is sweet, understanding. She speaks in a low voice while leading me to the room, "Your grandmother has been unconscious since she arrived. It appears she suffered a heart attack while at home."

A heart attack. At first, I thought this might've been a bad fall. Peter hadn't been too descriptive over the phone, and Grandmother is getting up there in years. Older people fall. It can be extremely dangerous.

But a heart attack? Tears roll down my cheeks, and I can barely hear anything else the nurse says because my grandmother had a heart attack and she could have died—and she might still die for all I know.

What am I supposed to do without her?

The room is small, walled off by glass. Easier for the staff to look inside at the patients who need the most help, I would think. It's crazy, the things that go through a person's head when they're fighting against the impulse to dissolve into tears.

There she is. Lying there, hooked up to a million machines. I have to remind myself to move my feet before approaching her bed. Everything takes an effort. Gosh, this is so surreal. Like it's happening to somebody else. Not to me.

Not to her.

"Grandmother"—her hand is so small in mine, and my hands are already pretty small—"I'm here."

The only answer comes from the beeping of machines monitoring her pulse, her blood pressure, all of that. I don't know what any of it means, the readouts on the screens over her head, but I guess it's okay. There aren't any alarms going off or anything like that.

Gosh, she looks so frail in the bed. So … old.

It hurts me to think it, and I know she'd hate it if

she knew the thought so much as passed through my mind. But it's the truth. She looks old. Because she is old. Sure, she's vibrant and energetic and sharp-witted. She has a dirty mind and an even dirtier sense of humor.

But she's in her mid-seventies, and I can't forget it. I can't let myself become complacent, to assume she'll always be around.

That's the thing about being in the hospital. All of the little disguises and masks a person uses to conceal what's going on underneath, they fade away under harsh fluorescent lights.

"Oh, you're here. I know she would be happy." Peter slowly enters the room, taking a place at the other side of the bed.

He has a chair pulled up beside the bed so he can be near her in case she needs anything.

"I'm so happy you're here with her," I whisper with a smile. "What happened?"

He runs a hand over his thin gray hair before shrugging. "She was her normal self this evening. A few of her friends came by for their pinochle game. She enjoyed herself and seemed to be in fine spirits when she retired. I'd only settled in to sleep when I heard her fall upstairs."

"Oh no." To think, if he had been sleeping, he might've missed it. And she might've stayed that way. "Was she conscious?"

"Yes, at first, she was. I called for an ambulance, and she fell unconscious before the paramedics arrived." There's a tightness in his voice and a tremor. He's upset. Deeply.

"I'm so glad she had you there to look after her. She's so lucky to have you. Has she ever told you so? How lucky she is, I mean."

He favors me with a genuine smile. "Does that sound like something she would say?"

"Good point."

We share a soft laugh.

"No, she hasn't. She isn't the sort of person to express such sentiments. That has never been the way of our relationship."

"I understand." *But do I?* There's something in the way he's looking at her, the way he tucks the blanket a little tighter around her sleeping form. "How long have you been working for her? I can't even remember. Since before I was born, right?"

"Thirty-four years." There's a note of pride in his voice.

I can imagine he'd be proud. She can't be an easy person to work for.

"That's a long time." Again, I notice the way he smooths out her blanket, the way he plumps the pillow under her head. Even though she doesn't know he's doing it, he's making sure she's comfortable.

Dear Lord, how did I not see it before now? No way he's been with her for more than three decades without developing an attachment. You don't live under the same roof with a person, serving their meals and taking care of them, without becoming attached.

Without maybe loving them.

No wonder he still works for her at his age. He's roughly her age. This is the age when people retire. Not when they continue overseeing cooking and serving and turning down the bedding and making sure their boss has everything she's become accustomed to after living a life of having things her way.

"You really care about her, don't you? Don't worry," I whisper when he looks surprised. "I won't tell."

His face works like he's trying to figure out what to say. How much he should say. Heck, maybe he's never considered it before now. *Is that possible? Can a person go through their day-to-day life, one task after another, without looking at the bigger picture and seeing what's been happening in their heart all along?*

When Peter speaks, it's slowly and with great care, "I don't think a man can look after a woman like your grandmother as long as I have without developing ... a fondness."

"Of course not. You're only human."

"She wouldn't like hearing us talk about this." He looks bashful, turning his gaze away from me.

"It's a good thing she can't hear us then." I reach over to pat his hand, where it's resting on the other side of Grandmother's legs. "Besides, if there's one thing I've learned as a writer, it's feelings. Emotions. You can't walk around with this inside you and never talk about it."

I can't imagine he has a lot of people in his life to share this with. One of the things that's always made him an excellent butler is how completely available he is to Grandmother at any time of the day or night. He even drives her around when she needs him to.

We sit in silence for a while, both of us lost in thought. *Is it possible he hasn't considered in all this time how he feels about her?* Maybe. Or maybe he's wondering if he's ever made it obvious. Whether she knows.

I could tell him with a pretty high degree of certainty that Grandmother has no idea he has feelings for her. I love her, but she's not the woman who pays attention to that sort of thing. Not from her loyal butler—aka somebody not in her social circle.

Knowing her, if she were awake right now, she'd make a case in favor of turning a construction worker into her boy toy. That would be just fine.

But an emotional relationship with a servant? Gasp. The horror.

"How are you holding up?" I finally think to ask after sitting in silence for a long, long time. I don't even know how long I've been here anymore. There's a clock on one of the many monitors over Grandmother's head, telling me it's been over an hour with no developments.

At least she doesn't look to be in destress. I'm happy to see her resting quietly.

Peter lifts a shoulder, but he can't fool me. He looks plain worn out. There's a gray tinge to his face and a droop to his eyes. "I'm holding up," is all he tells me.

"You should go home and get some sleep."

Another shoulder lift. At least he looks at me this time when he replies, "There's a pull-out sofa under the window." He points to it. "I'll be fine here, I assure you."

"I'm sure she wouldn't want to see you getting sick because of this." When that doesn't get a reaction, I try a different tactic. "Somebody's going to have to take care of her when she wakes up and gets better and goes home. She'll still be weak and in need of rest. If you aren't up to the task …"

"I'll be up to the task. I've looked after your grandmother for many years. I know what it takes. If this means a little extra effort, a little extra attention, so be it. Whatever she needs."

He then closes one hand over hers, and something about that simple gesture brings tears to my eyes.

This is love. This is devotion. I've never seen anything like it—at least, not since I've grown up. I'm sure my parents were loving and tender toward each other, but I was too young to notice or care. Kids generally feel icky about watching their parents be tender with each other, don't they?

The thing here is, there's nothing in it for him. She doesn't love him back. He takes care of her, and she simply provides compensation for that care. That's enough to keep him by her side, treating her with tenderness, even when she is unconscious and has no idea.

Or maybe it's because she has no idea since, now, she can't tell him to stop fussing over her. Which she definitely would if she were conscious.

"Kathryn?" There's excitement in Peter's voice. "She moved her hand."

I sit up, watching, waiting. Am I breathing? I don't know. All I know is, her eyelids are fluttering and her hands are moving and she's mumbling something incoherent.

"Grandmother? Can you hear me? Say something if you can, please." I look from her to Peter, where he's hovering over her, and it just about breaks my heart to see how eager he is.

There's an entire lifetime of love in his eyes. *Gosh, how did I never see it until now?*

How has she never?

Her eyes open slowly. "I hear you," she whispers. "I don't see why you have to holler at me that way, but I hear you."

And the fact that she sounds exactly like she always has is what breaks the dam and starts me crying all over again.

Chapter Sixteen

"THAT WON'T HAPPEN *anymore.*" She threw a look over her shoulder while pulling on her cardigan. "Don't even bother thinking it will."

"You've said that before. Twice, I think." He pulled on his jeans, watching her. The way she moved, the way she threw her hair over one shoulder before looking down to button her sweater. Hair he'd just had his hands in, pulling and twisting it around his fingers while her head moved up and down …

If he wasn't careful, he'd end up with a hell of a hard-on and no one to take care of it.

While he had no doubt they'd be doing this over and over again, he doubted he'd get lucky so soon. They would go through their usual dance. She would ignore him for a couple days. He'd reach out and get a quick one-worded answer. He'd reach out repeatedly, coaxing her out of her shell until they were back at his place again.

Or her place. Or his truck. Wherever.

So long as he was with her, deep inside her, with only her scent and her taste and her touch all over him. There was no comparison to that thrill, that charge. Guys in his line of work liked to pretend they didn't get a charge from *running into a fire while everybody else ran out.*

They were full of shit.

"Fine. But this time, I mean it. We can't keep doing this." She pulled on her boots and stood, straightening out her clothes, combing her hair with her fingers.

It didn't matter how she tried to make it look like she hadn't gotten fucked—and hard. She could put herself back together and swipe on a fresh coat of lip gloss, and the rest of the world might think she was the cute, cheerful teacher who never so much as uttered an angry word.

He knew better.

UGH. THIS ISN'T *very good.* At least, it's not flowing smoothly.

I can't even remember when I first sat down in front of the laptop today. The light has changed since then, though it wasn't exactly sunny in the first place. One of those days when it keeps threatening to snow, but nothing ever quite starts up.

My neck is stiff. My jaw hurts from grinding my teeth—wow, sometimes I'm super literal. Grinding out my work while grinding my teeth.

Silly me, thinking that throwing myself into work would help me get over worrying about Grandmother. Sure, it's awesome that she woke up and sounded just like her old self. She was salty with the doctors and nurses, even with me and Peter.

Only when a very stern, very assertive doctor

put it to her straight did she change her tune. *"You had a heart attack. You were unconscious for hours and are barely strong enough to lift your head from your pillow. We don't keep patients in the ICU when they aren't sick."*

I almost asked for his phone number. Not because I wanted to check in with him on my grandmother's condition. But because that was the only time I'd ever seen her shut up so fast, with such little effort. That's the sort of power I want to have at my fingertips.

Still, even though she seemed to be doing well by the time I left the hospital, that doesn't mean I can stop wondering what I'd be doing right now if things had gone differently. If Peter hadn't heard her fall. If the heart attack had been more severe.

She thinks me inheriting her wealth once she's gone will make up for her absence in my life. We've already had that discussion in the not-too-distant past, and it makes my nose wrinkle in disgust just as much as it did back then. Like any dollar amount would replace her.

Facts are still facts. She's okay—or she will be. And I'm okay too.

Which means I absolutely have to get back to work. Time is ticking by, and I have to submit my final edits by the holidays, so my first draft has to be in Maggie's hands well before that.

My characters are doing well. At least, once my heroine loosens up a little, they'll be doing well.

She's still guarding herself against the feelings her firefighter hero stirs in her heart … and her loins.

My hero? He knows she'll be his in the end. What he doesn't know is how close he'll come to death and how he never realized until meeting her as an adult and becoming intimate with her that it hadn't mattered before whether he lived or died.

It matters very much now. She'll be the last thing he thinks about before a roof collapses on him and his fellow firefighters. That's when he'll know for sure this isn't just a case of lust. That's when he'll know he loves her, that nobody else will ever take her place.

It just so happens that's when she'll figure she loves him too.

How neat things are in my books—in romance books on the whole. We guarantee a happy ending. That's one of the tenets of romance. There has to be a happy ending.

Real life? That's a whole other beast.

The knock at my front door comes as a surprise, especially when I know Matt's out of town, visiting family. He took Phoebe with him, so I don't even have her to keep me company. Or to complain to, which I tend to do when she and I are alone.

What can I say? She's an excellent listener.

I tiptoe to the door just in case it's a sicko or a weirdo. You never know when they'll show up, even in a nicer part of town like this one.

It's not a sicko or a weirdo. At least, I hope Bryce

isn't either of those things.

I swing the door open with a smile and am deeply glad I took the time to give myself a blowout this morning after my post-workout shower. "Hey you."

Holy cow. Now, with the door open, I have a full view of him.

The man looks good enough to eat, even in his work clothes. The long-sleeved shirt looks like it was painted over his bulging shoulders and biceps. It doesn't help that I can't stop thinking about him in his gear after watching him get ready to go out on a call.

My hormones are on overdrive, in other words, and the man is going to slip in a puddle of my drool if I don't get myself under control.

His hands are behind his back, and there's a playful grin he's trying hard to hide. "Hi, beautiful. I know you said things turned out okay last night, but I wanted to drop by and see how you were holding up before I went in today."

"You're too much. You're also hiding some-thing. What is it?"

Amazing how my spirits have lifted and all because he's standing in front of me. There's nothing like that early-in-a-relationship feeling. The rush of endorphins when the person you like appears in front of you. How everything they do seems so stinking cute.

"Oh, you mean, you think I'm hiding something

behind my back? Is that what you think?" He sidesteps me when I try to take a peek and then feints in the other direction to tease me. "You wanna see what I'm hiding?"

"I will attack you if you don't let me see!" Again, I try to jump behind him, but he's too fast.

"Is that supposed to be a threat? Am I supposed to want to avoid you attacking me?"

He's like a brick wall, his feet planted, totally immovable. I grab onto his shoulders and try reaching behind him, but that's a waste of time. He's too tall, and my arms aren't long enough.

"You might be surprised how strong I am," I growl.

"I wasn't talking about strength." He's wearing a sexy grin as he finally gives in and reveals what he's been hiding—a gift bag holding two bouquets and a teddy bear. "One of them is for you. The other bouquet and the bear are for your grandmother. I know she's too old for teddy bears, but—"

Anything else he's about to say dies when I throw my arms around his neck and plant a big, wet kiss on his full mouth. He lets out a little grunt of surprise but recovers quickly, wrapping his arms around my waist and pulling me closer.

By the time we come up for air, I seriously wish he didn't have to go to work. And judging by the soft groan in my ear when he nuzzles my neck, I'm thinking he feels the same way.

"We'll have to pick up where we left off yesterday," he whispers before nipping at my earlobe.

I can't help but shiver a little. "Agreed. What are you thinking?"

"Hmm." He pulls back, looking down at me with a thoughtful expression. "I'm working a full twenty-four-hour shift starting today, and I'll probably be useless tomorrow night. What about Tuesday?"

I want to say yes, but the laptop behind me has other ideas. "You know what? I should really focus on work this week. I have to get this first draft to my editor and give her at least a workweek to get through it before revising. What about Friday? How does that look for you?"

His disappointment is obvious, but he shrugs anyway. "Friday night would be great. I'm off Saturday, so I'll be able to stay up late. If, you know, you're into the idea."

Am I into the idea?

Right now, with his hands on my hips and our bodies pressed together, with my lips still tingling a little, I can only nod enthusiastically. "I'm into the idea."

His smile is absolutely wicked. "Good."

"And by the way"—I know he's probably running late by now, but there's something I have to get off my chest—"my schedule's not always like this. But with the holidays coming up and people taking off—"

"I get it. I swear." He kisses the tip of my nose

before freeing himself from my arms. "And in a way, my schedule's just as crazy."

"How so?" I ask as we walk to the door.

"It's a shame, but this is the time of year when fires are most common. Holiday lights, dry trees …"

"Right, of course. That's awful."

"Not trying to freak you out or anything." He kisses me once more before heading for the stairs at the end of the hall. "But it's worth warning you. I might not be able to hang out if I get called in unexpectedly."

I wave good-bye, hoping nothing comes up at the last minute. And not only because it would be a terrible tragedy, but also because I'm already looking forward to Friday night and would hate to miss the opportunity to be with him.

Should I ask if he can wear any of his equipment to my place, or would that be too much?

Chapter Seventeen

"I DON'T SEE why everyone is making such a fuss." Her sigh fills the otherwise quiet, private room.

Now that she's no longer in extreme danger, my grandmother has been moved out of the ICU and into a room of her own for observation.

And I'm sure nobody has ever received better care. She even has a mini refrigerator to keep her drinks cold and an electric teakettle for when she's in need of a little chamomile.

I can't help but roll my eyes and sigh a little. "Grandmother, you're in a hospital. In a bed. Because you had a heart attack."

"A mild heart attack, dear. Don't exaggerate."

"I'm not exaggerating." I take a seat in the chair next to her bed. "I was here not long after they brought you in. When you were unconscious. Because you had had a heart attack and were sick."

"Must you throw it in my face?"

"I'm not trying to throw anything in your face. Though now that we're on the topic, maybe it's time you start taking better care of yourself."

"This again." She rests her head against the pillows, looking up at the ceiling. Sitting in her bed, raised up the way she is, with her hair neatly combed and a touch of lipstick, she's more like the woman I've come to know and adore.

And need. Terribly.

"Yes, this again. Maybe it's time to cool it with the afternoon cocktails. And the evening cocktails too. And your diet could use a little work."

"Pardon me, but I eat very well."

"You eat foods full of sodium and saturated fat. Peter told me so."

"Peter?" She groans. "The traitor. Telling tales behind my back."

"He's going to start preparing healthier foods, whether you like it or not."

"I don't like it one bit."

"I realize that. So does he. But that's the way it has to be. Grandmother," I insist when she mutters what sounds suspiciously like a foul curse, "we both want you to be around for a long, long time. We're not ready to get along without you yet."

"That much I believe. I don't know what either of you would do without me."

"At least you're sounding more like yourself." I wave my arms around the room, indicating the almost-obscene number of floral arrangements. "And we're not the only people who couldn't do without you, in case an entire church full of flowers isn't enough proof."

She purses her lips, eyes narrowing. "Or a funeral home."

"Grandmother."

"Those catty bitches only want to see me six feet under, so they can be queen bee or top dog or whatever they want to call it."

"You're too hard on them."

That gets me a withering look.

"I've known them a lot longer than you have, my dear. I know what I'm talking about. They don't care the first thing about whether I make it out of this hospital alive."

"Well, I do." I close a hand over hers. "Very much. I don't want to lose you. Okay?"

"Dear, odds are, you will. I'll go before you will."

"I'm not ready. I'm not. I need you."

She scoffs. "You've done very well without me."

"Why are you so determined to tell me I don't feel the way I feel? Is it that hard to accept that you're my last living family member and I'd be completely lost without you?"

She allows a tiny smile. "I don't doubt you'd be lost."

"There you go. That's the attitude I expected."

"What about you?" She fixes me with one of her patented appraising stares.

"What about me?"

"How've you been? It's been more than two weeks since the auction, but we haven't had the opportunity to talk about what came of it. Did you sink a knife into that bastard's back?"

Boy, she's feeling feisty today. Must be all the rest she's gotten.

"Not yet. No, I don't think that'll ever happen. We've gotten past it."

"I knew you would."

"You're very wise."

"Smirk all you want, young lady, but I know you. I know my granddaughter. You have a sweet, generous heart, and you don't hold a grudge."

"That's where you're wrong."

"Oh, you might tell yourself you're holding a grudge, but you don't. When push comes to shove, you're a reasonable, kind person who wants to smooth things over as soon as possible."

"You make me sound like a pushover. And if you don't mind, I'm taking my hand back."

She holds on tighter than ever. The woman's darn strong for somebody who had a heart attack, but that shouldn't come as a surprise. She's always been stronger than she looks. Only a real fool would mistake her for a weakling just because she's petite and getting on in years.

"Not until you tell me what I want to know. And you're no pushover, my dear. Don't mistake me on that."

"Because I sort of feel like one now. I mean, now that you mention it, I rolled over and agreed when my editor told me the type of books I needed to write. Even though I didn't want to."

"That isn't being a pushover. That's an example of someone who can change course when they know they need to. A tactical maneuver. Not weakness."

"If you say so."

"You saved your career because you weren't too stubborn to change course at the advice of a professional. Yes, dear granddaughter, I do say so."

"Okay, you've made your point." I can't help but feel a little overwhelmed when she puts it that way. "Why is it that we can always see things about other people's lives and not our own?"

"I don't have to listen to your inner voice in my head all day long, don't forget."

"Lucky you. It can be a real nightmare in there."

"So? Bryce? What happened with him?"

I finally withdraw my hand and lean back in my chair. I feel this is going to be a long visit, so I might as well get comfortable. "Our relationship is progressing, I think."

"You think? What does that mean?"

"It means, I should hate him and want to watch him burn, but instead, I've been out with him several times, and I have plans to see him tomorrow."

"That's nice. I'm glad you worked things out. He's gorgeous, isn't he?"

"Just a little." I hold up my thumb and forefinger, maybe a quarter of an inch between them. "He seems like a genuine person too. He's grown up considerably. You should've seen him with the kids when he dressed as Santa during a party they had at the firehouse. It was incredibly sweet. And those flowers and the teddy bear are from him." I point them out, almost lost among the rest of the plant life taking up more space than her bed does.

"You seem slightly smitten with him."

"I didn't want to be. Does that sound wrong?"

"No. It sounds honest. And I will never be unhappy to hear you speak honestly."

"Except when I'm telling you how to eat and to stop drinking so much."

"Naturally, because those things happen to do with me, and I don't like being told what to do." If she were a clam, she'd close her shell tight at the mention of the lifestyle changes she needs to make. Folding her hands over her covered lap, she informs me, "Peter has another thing coming if he believes he's in any position to tell me what to do."

I clear my throat at the mention of his name. This could either go well or ridiculously bad. Either/or. Fifty-fifty. I don't love my odds, but I think something needs to be said. She deserves to know.

"Remember what we were just talking about?" I venture, leaning in a little.

"Kathryn, I had a mild heart attack. I don't have dementia. Of course I remember."

"So, you remember that whole part about other people being able to see things better than we can since they're standing outside a situation and can see the big picture? This isn't the first time we've talked about that recently, is it?"

"You're right. Though I don't see why you're bringing this up."

Here goes nothing. "I think it's time to consider Peter caring about you as more than an employer."

Her face goes completely blank for a second, which scares the ever-living heck out of me. *Did I kill her? Was that too much for her heart to handle?*

When she bursts out laughing, I don't know if I'm relieved or annoyed. "Peter? Oh, come now."

"Grandmother, are you honestly telling me you don't see how he could've come to care about you over the years?"

"I'm his employer! He works for me!" She waves a dismissive hand, shaking her head, still chuckling like this is the best joke she's heard in ages.

It doesn't dissuade me. It angers me. "I'm disappointed in you."

Her laughter dies instantly. "Excuse me?"

"You heard me. You had a heart attack. You didn't go deaf."

Color blazes on her cheeks. "Young lady, you will speak to me with respect."

"I just told you something somebody else told me in confidence, hoping it would convince you to change your attitude toward them or at least consider their feelings, and you laughed about it.

That's downright cruel. I never imagined you were cruel. Difficult, yes. Demanding, yes. But cruel?"

I'm on my feet with my purse over one shoulder by the time she stops me.

"Wait. Wait, please." She holds out her hands, though it's not like she could stop me that way if I was determined to leave.

It's the tremor in her voice that brings me to a halt and turns me in place.

"What is it?"

Her eyes dart back and forth over my face, her brow furrowed. "Who told you that in confidence?"

"Peter," I whisper. "Who do you think? He told me so the night you came in here, when you had the attack. He sat next to you, made sure you were covered up and comfortable. I don't think he left until after you woke up, did he?"

She blinks rapidly. "I—that is, he was by my bed when I woke up. I remember that. There was a great deal of confusion, but I remember seeing him. And then you."

"I know. We were here together. He didn't leave your side. I encouraged him to go, to sleep since you'll probably need even more help once you get home and he needs to rest up for that. He refused. He wouldn't leave your side."

She leans back, almost deflating. "Well … I mean … that's to be expected. He's been by my side for a long time. He's accustomed to it."

"Grandmother, get real." I pull the chair closer

this time and sit next to her. "Like I just said, he told me so. In confidence, yes, but I thought you should know. Maybe you could be a little nicer to him."

"He told you?"

"He did."

"He … cares for me?" She stares at the wall beyond the foot of the bed. "He told you he does?"

"He told me he does. He's been with you for so long. Of course he was going to feel close to you after a while. He takes your health seriously. He takes your well-being seriously. I mean, think about it."

"I am. I am." Her voice is soft, far away.

I almost feel bad for how confused she looks and sounds even though I think she's blind for not having known this before. I mean, granted, I just now figured it out, but she *had* to know.

When she looks at me again, her eyes shine with what I realize are unshed tears. "You have to understand something. In my world, the way I was brought up, servants are one class, and we're in another. I never considered him developing feelings for me."

"He's practically your live-in boyfriend."

"Kathryn." She clicks her tongue in disappointment. "I'm experiencing a revelation, and you think this is a time to make jokes."

"I'm not making jokes. In a way, that's how the two of you live. You sit and read the paper on Sunday mornings over coffee and muffins. He goes to concerts and plays with you whenever you have an extra ticket. He cooks your meals and eats many of them with you. He cleans up after you; you provide for him. I mean, come on. You two are closer than a lot of couples I know—and you get along better too."

"Are you trying to talk me into having an affair with my butler?" The woman looks downright horrified.

"No. I'm trying to talk you into seeing what's right in front of you. Don't be a snob. For once, look past your patrician nose and see what's there. Don't talk yourself out of anything just because he's a servant. That's all I want. And for heaven's sake, be kind to him."

"I can do that much," she offers.

I can tell this has knocked her sideways, poor thing. She really had no idea. Now, I bet she'll spend the rest of the day looking back over every little conversation, every memory, seeing it through different eyes.

It'll be better if she's alone for that.

"I'll see you later. Be nice to the nurses."

She barely gives me a distracted wave in reply.

Chapter Eighteen

"KITTY, MY DARLING girl, I don't think you've ever submitted your first draft ahead of schedule."

I wait for her to continue, but Maggie's not in the mood to be more forthcoming, I guess. "Thank you? Is that a good thing?"

"It's a wonderful thing!"

Good, because I darn near killed myself to get it to her so early. I barely slept, ate, or changed my clothes from the time I got home from visiting Grandmother on Sunday afternoon until I sent the draft over to Maggie on Wednesday night.

I then spent most of Thursday in what I like to think of as a waking coma. Time passed. I was awake for most of it but not exactly active.

I considered decorating for Christmas but could barely bring myself to get off the couch.

Matt came home at some point, but even the sound of Phoebe scratching at my door wasn't enough to get me moving. I'm sure she'll forgive me.

It's Friday now, meaning I should get to see Bryce tonight.

Which means I've spent the morning cleaning the apartment in that special way a person does when they think there's a good chance they won't be spending the night alone. Clean sheets, clean bathroom, clean everything. I want him to come away from this with a good impression of me, obviously.

And wanting to come back again too. Which is why I don't understand men who don't bother cleaning before a woman comes over. Like … do they ever want to have a repeat visit?

Maybe they don't. Maybe that's the whole point.

Maybe I've thought way too much about this.

"So, what do you think of what you've read?"

This is always the worst part. The very worst. It's like putting my beating heart out there in the world and asking somebody to step on it. Instantly, I doubt every word I wrote.

Every word I've ever written in fact.

"I think your sex scenes are much hotter, just the way I wanted them!" She even cheers a little. I can hear clapping in the background. "I mean, I sincerely felt the hatred Nina felt for Larsen in the beginning. But I could see how she fell for him too. He was so sexy and irresistible but so generous and brave. The perfect man."

I have to bite my lip to hold back a giggle. If I laugh or show any glee at all, she'll take it as me thinking of the man who Larsen is based on. Which means she won't let me get off the phone until I spill my guts.

As it turns out, my self-control is all for nothing. I should've known.

"You do realize that you have to tell me all about the guy who inspired this character."

"Maggie, I just completed a first draft for you in under three weeks. Can you give me a minute to breathe before you start asking personal questions?"

"Ooh, so he's realer than I thought," she murmurs.

"What makes you say that?"

"If you made him up, you would tell me so."

Darn it. "I don't want to talk about him. Please. He's a nice guy, and that's that."

"A nice guy who saves lives for a living."

"That's also true."

"Who you hated at some point …" The amount of hope in her voice is actually pretty sad.

There are times when I want to ask whether she has a life and whether she's happy with it. *Why is she so obsessed with my life?*

"I don't want to talk about it anymore, and I know you're going to interpret that however you see fit."

"Well, regardless of any of that, if he was enough to rouse this much creativity, he's all right with me. I swear, I need a new pair of panties."

And there it is. I knew she wouldn't be able to finish without delivering one truly gagworthy comment.

"I'll take that as a sign of a job well done." I swear, the woman is determined to embarrass me to death.

"Aside from a few notes here and there— nothing too serious—I don't have much to say about it. You're getting better at this with each book."

"Really?"

"Since when have I blown smoke up your ass?"

That's Maggie—blunt as ever. I don't have the heart to remind her of how she fawned over me when I was on the best-seller list for my sweet romances.

"It's just that I don't feel that way. Like I'm getting better."

"You're improving with each book. I mean that. Especially considering how much resistance you felt at first."

She's got me there. If I hadn't finally gotten over my phobia about writing on-trend romance, I would either have no career by now or I'd be a full-blown alcoholic. I could barely stand the thought of writing a sexy scene without getting drunk.

And then I ended up getting too drunk to write or even stay conscious. So, I'd be back in No Careersville, where I'd never write another intelligible word again.

"I appreciate your support. I know it's been a difficult year, and I didn't make it easy at first, but having you on my side has meant a lot. You didn't have to tell me to keep writing. You could've let the publisher drop me. So, thanks."

"Oh, Kitty. That means a great deal. Thank you." For the first time in our working relationship, it sounds like Maggie's a little choked up.

Which means it's time to get off the phone. I'm sure by the time I read her notes, I won't feel quite so warm toward her anyway, so it's better to leave this sentimental moment where it is.

And that's fine since I heard somebody come in from a walk just a minute ago, and I want to let him know I'm alive before he calls the authorities for a wellness check.

"I've gotta go, Maggie."

"Bye, Kitty. I'll be waiting for those edits," she says in her usual clear voice.

Phoebe just about tackles me when Matt answers the door.

"She's alive!" he croaks, walking with his arms outstretched like an old-timey horror movie villain.

"Frankenstein's monster walked that way, but he didn't say that. Gosh, get your quotes straight."

He rolls his eyes. "It's easy to forget how much fun you are."

"Thanks for heeding the note I slid under your door." I follow him into his apartment and grab one of Phoebe's tug-of-war ropes since she's clearly dying to play.

"Did I have a choice?" he asks before reciting

what I wrote. *"If you bother me before I submit this draft, I will kill you. I won't wait until you're asleep. I'll do it when you're awake and aware."*

"What can I say? I was desperate to finish up."

"And now that you have, how are you feeling?"

"Not awful." Phoebe takes hold of the other end of the rope and just about takes my arm off. "Hey, girl, I need to type for a living!"

"You could always dictate," Matt suggests while his dog continues pulling until I have to give up and let go.

"Wow. She's strong." I rub my shoulder while giving a rueful grin. "That's what I get for trying to play and make up for lost time."

He's got a nice, rosy glow going on.

"Only you could get a tan while visiting family during the winter." I sigh.

"I never said I was visiting them someplace cold. Actually, my brother rented a house in Florida. That's where we were."

"You were in Florida?"

"You were working anyway, so what difference does it make where we were?"

He has a point.

"You at least had fun, I hope?"

"Sure." He's smiling in a warm, genuine way when he sits on the couch to watch us play. "It's always fun, hanging out with my niece and nephew. They're a great time. They're also exhausting. This one over here is used to being played with pretty intensely after the last several days." He reaches out to scratch Phoebe's ears.

"No wonder she's feeling so rambunctious."

"Speaking of rambunctious ..." He sits back with a groan. "We never talked about my date."

It's like an early Christmas present. I totally forgot he even had a date after the auction. And now, he's being generous enough to open up about it without my begging, and he sounds sort of regretful.

I'm so glad I visited. Pulled shoulder muscles be damned.

"What happened?" I can't even pretend to be less interested than I am.

"You sorta look like Phoebe does when I bring out the treat bag."

"Tell me. Tell me. Tell me. Tell me."

He covers his ears with his hands. "My niece does that when she wants to know something. Only she's six years old."

"This would all be over if you'd just tell me what happened on your date."

I know it couldn't have gone well or else he'd be bragging about it.

"You know your grandmother's friend Whitney?"

"Yeah?"

"Imagine her, like, fifty years ago."

"Oh. No."

"Oh, yeah. I'm surprised she didn't ask for a

copy of my latest tax return, so she could verify my income. When she wasn't talking about how much her family owns, she was doing charming things, like running her foot up my leg under the table and asking if I had any nudes on my phone."

"Shut up."

"I won't."

"She asked you that?"

"She did."

"What did you say?"

He stops for a second, looking at me like I'm crazy. "I said no."

"I was only wondering. I guess there won't be a second date."

"There will not. I didn't even get a BJ out of it."

"It sounds like she would've been all about it though, right?"

Again with the look he's giving me. "I do have standards, you know. One mouth isn't the same as any other."

I can't help but respect that. He's not quite the shameless slut I used to think he was, back when all I knew about him was how many times a week he made women scream in his bedroom.

Though I would never actually tell him that. Instead, I sigh and bat my eyelashes. "Wow. You're such a poet."

Chapter Nineteen

THIS IS IT.

This is it.

This is the night. I can feel it.

No matter what anybody says to the contrary, there's a whole lot hanging in the balance. The first night together is an important one. It sets the tone for the nights that will follow.

Or maybe I'm overthinking this. It wouldn't be the first time I've overthought something.

Everything's as perfect as I can make it. When I texted Bryce earlier today, he said it would be great if we ordered food and ate it at my place. It's all ready, waiting in a warm oven.

Are the candles too much? I don't think so. I hope not anyway. If I'd had the time to go downstairs to the storage unit, I could've brought up my strings of lights and hung them around the apartment. That would've been sweet and romantic, not to mention holiday-themed. But there wasn't time. The candles will have to do.

I'm definitely overthinking this.

It's just that out of the handful of men I've dated

lately, Bryce seems like the most likely candidate for a serious relationship. He's perfect boyfriend material. Granted, if anybody had told me when I was a kid that I'd ever think anything even remotely like this, I would've …

I don't know what I would've done. Cried maybe. Because he made me that miserable.

That was then. Now, my palms are sweaty, and I'm only marginally sure I remembered to put on deodorant—and oh, of course, now is when there's a knock at the door, and I don't have time to dart back to my room to do a quick swipe.

Bryce doesn't seem to notice how discombobulated I feel when I open the door, which either means I'm doing a good job of covering or he's oblivious.

"There's the most beautiful thing I've seen in days." He smiles as he walks into the apartment.

"I hope you're talking about me and not the candles."

"I was definitely not talking about the candles." He wraps me up in a tight hug. "You have no idea how much I've been looking forward to this. I swear, the thought of seeing you tonight is what got me through."

Oh. That doesn't sound good.

I have to bend backward and crane my neck to get a look at him. "What's that mean? What happened?"

He lets me go with a sigh. "I wasn't going to say

anything. I don't want to bring you down. I told myself I didn't want to ruin tonight."

Well, there goes the romance for now.

"It's okay. If something is bothering you, let's talk about it. Are you hungry? The food's waiting."

"I knew you weren't the only good-smelling thing in the apartment." He waits for me in front of the coffee table while I carry in platters of rice, chicken, tofu, and noodles. It's a good thing he likes Chinese food as much as I do.

"So, let's talk about it. What happened?" I pour us each a glass of wine while he puts a plate together for himself.

"I figured you wouldn't have heard about it since you've been working so hard all week." He rubs the back of his neck and rolls his head from side to side like he's feeling tension. "There were two big fires this week. I was on-site for both of them."

"Oh no. You're right; I had no idea." It never occurred to me to pay closer attention. I was neck deep in my book.

"It's okay. I didn't think you would."

"Do you want to talk about the fires? Or anything else?"

"House fires. Faulty wiring on the one, a burning tree on the other. Like I said, this time of year is the worst. And don't even get me started on what happens when people use space heaters and fall asleep without making sure they aren't touching anything flammable."

Wow. This evening is going in a vastly different direction than I expected. Then again, I might be the only person he feels comfortable talking with about this sort of thing. Men don't usually sit around, sharing feelings, and he's surrounded by men all day.

"I'm so sorry. That must be hard to leave behind at the end of a shift."

"It's practically impossible sometimes. So, I'm a little off at the moment. But just a little," he insists when he looks at my face.

I mean, I'm frowning on the inside, so it only makes sense that disappointment would show on the outside.

I really should start paying more attention to local news. Though I also know myself, which means I know I'd obsess and worry about every-thing.

Crap. Now, I'm really getting depressed. Of course, my imagination won't let me leave things where they are. God forbid.

What would it be like, being Bryce's girlfriend?
How many ulcers would I end up with?

"I'm sorry." He reaches out, stroking my cheek. "Let's talk about your work. You submitted your draft early. What did your editor think?"

"She thinks if I used you to inspire my hero, you're the perfect man."

Poor Bryce almost shoots rice out of his nose.

"Hardly!" he chokes as I pat him on the back. Once he's finished choking, he shoots me a withering look. "Don't do that to me when I have a mouth full of food."

"I didn't know you'd burst out laughing!"

"What else am I supposed to do? Say, *Oh, yeah, I'm super perfect. She's so right.*" He rolls his eyes, still chuckling as he goes back to his fried rice.

"Hey, you're pretty perfect. Just because you can't accept that doesn't make it untrue."

"You're the one calling me perfect? Please." He looks me up and down with those dangerous, dark eyes. They're so bright in the candlelight. "You're the total package. Beautiful, successful, but not full of yourself. Warm, sweet, smart. You don't fall for just any line, but you have an open heart. I mean, how much more perfect can a woman get?"

"What are you trying to do? Make me forget all about dinner?"

He shrugs with a wicked grin. "Maybe. Or maybe I'm telling you the truth. It's the truth, no matter what we're doing—eating dinner or otherwise. You're everything I've ever wanted."

Maybe he's not quite as depressed as he seemed before. Otherwise, being with me is enough to lift his spirits. I don't want to let it go to my head, but how am I supposed to avoid it?

He leaves his plate on the table, turning to me. Our knees touch. "You went to all this trouble tonight. I can't explain what it means to me to come here to you, to this. After looking forward to it all week, to see you and know you cared so much about making tonight special … it means the world."

If I didn't know better, I'd think he was trying to get me to fall in love with him.

Heck, I might not know better. He might really be trying it. And he might be succeeding.

"You deserve somebody who makes you feel that way. I'm glad it can be me."

He reaches for me, stroking my cheek again. This time, rather than letting his hand fall away, he slides it around to the back of my neck and pulls me a little closer. I get the feeling he's not interested in dinner anymore.

For that matter, neither am I. I can eat whenever.

"I want it to be you." He touches his forehead to mine. "I know we started off badly. I know you didn't go into this wanting anything more than a date and a little research. You couldn't have even been in it for the sex since you already wrote your first draft and we haven't gotten past first base yet."

"You were rounding first and heading to second before the phone interrupted us," I remind him with a breathy laugh. My heart flutters at the thought.

"I want you to know that I'd like to keep seeing you. I'd like it so much." He kisses me softly, gently. "I want more of you in my life."

"Even though I can't skate?"

He laughs against my throat. "Even though you can't skate. I figured you were pretending at first, like you wanted the excuse to have me hold you. But nobody can pretend to be that bad."

"I'm not even offended."

We're both laughing when our lips meet again and again, each kiss deeper than the last, until dinner is the furthest thing from my mind.

Until there's nothing to do but get up and dart around the living room, blowing out the candles as I go.

"What are you doing?" Bryce asks as I plunge the room further into darkness with each candle I extinguish.

"I don't want to leave them burning while we're busy." When I reach him again, I hold out a hand. "It might be dangerous."

"All that, and she cares about fire safety too." He takes my hand and stands, following me to the bedroom. "I'm starting to think I could fall in love with you, Kitty Valentine."

Chapter Twenty

"THAT WAS IT? You stopped there?"

That's just like Hayley.

I'm sitting here, telling her all about what happened with Bryce, and all she wants to talk about is what didn't happen.

"I mean, we stopped where we stopped. At the perfect place, I think."

She frowns anyway. "Don't ask me why I care so much, but I was hoping you'd at least get laid by the time this was over."

"Wow. For one thing, who says it's over? Thanks for all your faith in me."

"Sorry." She points to her mug, where a boozy, holiday-themed coffee steams. "Too much holiday cheer."

"Sure." I roll my eyes to let her know what I think of that pitiful excuse. "Anyway, we both got something out of it. Believe. Me."

Her eyes light up again. "Oh, really? So, he was good …" She points to her crotch, eyes darting back and forth like she's afraid somebody at the restaurant will know what she's referring to.

"That is probably the classiest thing you've ever done, Hayley. Congratulations."

"I'm just saying. Was it good when he went downtown?"

"Went downtown? Even I've never used anything that lame in my books."

"Do you want me to get more graphic in front of people? Because you know I will. Your face will burst into flames by the time I'm finished."

"Okay, I get it. You don't have to do that."

"Because I will."

"I know you will. Jeez." I'm already blushing furiously as it is. "I've never loved talking about things like this. You know that."

"I know. Which is what makes your choice of career even more baffling sometimes."

"No, it doesn't. That's why I didn't write sexy scenes before now, duh." After taking a quick look around, I lean in and whisper, "It was extremely good. For a really, really long time."

"Ooh, yeah? Like, how long?"

"I didn't have a stopwatch handy, Hayley."

"Fine, fine." She leans across the table the way I am. "How many times did you …"

Again, I look around before holding up three fingers.

"I hate you!" she hisses, slamming her back against the booth. "I just hate you."

"Do not. Remember Timmy the Tongue? You were downright graphic when you described what went on with him, and you dated him for, what, four months?"

She sighs softly, staring out the window behind me. "Timmy. I wonder what he's up to nowadays."

"Focus." I snap my fingers in front of her. "You subjected me to that, and don't think it didn't make me jealous."

"You're right. You're due a little gloating."

"I wasn't trying to gloat …"

"You know what I mean. Gloat away, if you want to." Before I get the chance, she flashes a wicked smile. "What about Bryce?"

"What about him?" Oh, gee, my cheeks are hot again. Maybe hotter than before.

"Was he satisfied by the end of the night?"

"He sure seemed that way. And that's all I'm saying about it. After that, we snacked a little on what was left of dinner and went to sleep."

"Aww, he spent the night?" She crosses her hands over her chest with a sigh. "That's so nice."

"It was." I can't hold back a gleeful smile. "It really was. Just sleeping with somebody was nice. Especially somebody like him. He's not some jerk. He's not a random hook-up."

She rests her chin in her palm, elbows on the table. "So? What does this mean?"

"Does it have to mean anything?"

She scoffs.

"No, I'm serious," I insist. "I'm not trying to be cute. Does it have to mean anything? He spent the night. We messed around."

"It depends on how he feels, right? You've already told me how determined he seems to lock you down."

"You manage to make things sound so romantic."

"It's true though. And why wouldn't he wanna lock you down?" She tosses her golden hair back. "You're Kitty fucking Valentine. You're the whole package. Of course he's gonna pull out all the stops to make you his girlfriend."

"I don't think he's doing that yet. Dating exclusively maybe. But not boyfriend-girlfriend yet."

"Kitty, he went down on you until you came three times. And he spent the night. I bet you stayed up late talking, and then you cuddled the entire time you were asleep."

"So what if we did?" *And why am I suddenly shredding a napkin into teensy bits?*

"It's okay if he wants that. If you want it, I mean," she adds.

"I do want it. I think."

"Do me a favor and stop that." She covers my hands with hers before I get the chance to take her napkin and destroy it the way I've destroyed mine. "It's also okay if you don't want to be his girlfriend."

"I do though. I think I do. It's just that I don't know what that would do to my writing, for one thing."

"Please," she says, removing her hands and leaning back in the booth. "You can make things up however you need to. You don't absolutely have to date the guys you write about." She winks with a smirk. "Hey, think of it this way: you could tell him you need to write about all kinds of exciting, sexy things and you have to research with him."

"Hmm. Good point." Still, I can't help but wonder something. "Do you think he worked as hard as he did for as long as he did because I told him Maggie thought he was perfect and he wanted to put in a good performance for future writing inspiration?"

She giggles like crazy. "So what if he did? Hey, take your perks where you can get them."

"I guess." I have to giggle, too, but not as hard as she is. "I don't want him to feel too much pressure though. It can't be easy, dating a romance writer."

"You're always thinking about other people, aren't you?" She studies me with a patented Hayley squint, her head tipped to one side. "There's something else. I know you. You're thinking about something besides the pressure on him. What is it?"

"It's going to sound so shallow and terrible."

"I'll be the judge of that. You know I would never call you terrible, by the way."

I notice she doesn't include shallow, but I let it go. "I'm not sure I'm cut out to be a firefighter's girlfriend. I don't know if I could handle it."

Her mouth falls open. "Oh. I didn't think about that."

"Neither did I until last night." I share what Bryce told me about the fires he fought. "It would've been impossible to think about anything but whether he was okay. You know? I would've worried myself sick."

"I don't blame you," she admits with a sad frown. "I would've worried too."

"See what I mean? I can't ignore what he does. I'll be keeping an eye out all the time now whenever he's on duty—and probably when he isn't since he could be called in for a big fire."

"I'm sure it's rare for a firefighter to be seriously injured or worse," she offers. "I can't tell you the last time I heard of either thing happening, and I pay attention to the news."

"That's true. But you know me."

"You? The queen of overthinkers? The woman who has the most active imagination of anybody I know? The girl who, if given the choice between a positive possibility and the worst, most awful conclusion, would choose awful nine out of ten times?"

"Was that a prepared speech? Do you lie in bed at night, thinking of all the ways I suck?"

She offers a smile, taking my hands. "Hey. Relax, okay? If anything, this is the sort of thing people get used to. Partners, spouses. I'm sure it's the same for cops too. And soldiers. That doesn't mean they all spend their lives single. It's just that their loved ones learn to live with it. The worst might happen, but it rarely does."

By the time she's finished, I genuinely feel better. "I need to carry a pocket-sized version of you around with me wherever I go."

"You do. It's called having a phone. You know you're the only person in the world I answer the phone for instead of pretending I missed the call and texting an apology a few minutes later."

"I do know that. And vice versa."

"Thank you. So, you know you can call me anytime. No matter how busy I am."

"It's a shame I can't just marry you." I sigh, shaking my head. "But I'm not into you that way."

"One of nature's cruel jokes," she agrees with a mournful sigh.

Chapter Twenty-One

NOT LOVING THIS scene. Is there another way to wrap it up?

My head hurts. I rub my temples, glaring at Maggie's note. She made it sound like she only wanted simple changes, a little tweaking here and there.

She neglected to mention hating the final scene and wanting me to come up with something new. How convenient. I've been struggling with it, and now, it's the only thing I have left to revise before sending the new draft.

The ringing of my phone is a welcome distraction because, hey, any distraction during the writing or editing process is generally welcome.

"Where are you?" Hayley's question practically comes out as a shout.

"I'm at home." I have to pull the phone away from my ear and stare at it. "I'm editing, like I've been doing for days. What's wrong?"

"Turn on the news, babe."

There goes my stomach, plunging like I'm on a roller coaster and we just hit the first big hill. I minimize my document before pulling up the site for our local news channel.

"*Multi-alarm fire sweeps through warehouses in Garment District.*" I can barely breathe by the time I'm finished reading the headline.

"There's live video," she informs me as I'm already clicking the play button with a shaking hand. "Apparently, they called in companies from the other boroughs because this is such a huge fire."

"Sure. Warehouses, fabrics. It's gotta be terrible." I'm talking without thinking. Moving my mouth and making sounds come out. I can hardly even hear myself over the sickening thudding of my heart.

"I'm sure he's okay," she tells me as the video picks up.

I'm finally watching the live video feed.

"Oh my God, Hayley."

It's an inferno. There's what looks like an entire block of buildings on fire.

"I know. They said something about a problem with the hydrants around there. It took time to get them to work for some reason. I don't know. So, the firefighters lost time."

"I can't believe it."

"I'm sure he's okay," Hayley insists again. "I'm sure of it. They haven't said anything about injuries, so that's a good sign."

"True." I feel at least a small bit of relief when she puts it that way. "Hopefully, it stays that way."

"I'm sure it will. I probably should've waited until I wasn't so freaked before I called. I'm sorry."

"It's okay. I would've done the same thing."

We sit in silence, watching the news together. I don't know what I would do if it wasn't for her right now. I really don't.

"Have you tried to text him or anything?" she asks after a while.

"No. I figure he's not going to be able to use his phone if he's in the middle of fighting this thing."

"That's true, but you never know. He might have a minute. He might want to let you know he's okay, you know? Rather than leaving you hanging."

"Good point." I pull the phone away from my ear long enough to shoot him a text.

I'm watching the news. Please be careful. Let me know you're okay.

After I send it, I go back to Hayley. "You don't have to sit here on the phone with me. It's okay. This could last a long time—the size of it alone, you know?"

"I don't want you to have to watch this on your own."

"I'll be okay. So will he. There are a million fire-fighters out there right now. He's not working alone."

I wish I felt as confident as I'm trying to sound.

I also wish Jim's concerns about Bryce being reckless and rushing into danger would stop ringing through my memory.

Should I have said something about that to him before now? Should I have reminded him that I'm in his life now and I need him to take care of himself?

By the time an hour passes, the fire has spread to an office building attached to the string of warehouses. I would hope, by now, the building's empty since this fire's been going for a while. Even so, it's just another example of the fire not being under control. It's a windy day, which isn't helping.

"Just let him be okay." I don't know who I'm talking to or what I expect them to accomplish, but if there was ever a time for a prayer to be answered, this is it. "Just let him be okay."

It's almost midnight when one of the news anchors announces the fire is under control. There's relief in her voice. "We've received reports of minor injuries to several firefighters, who are currently being treated—"

"What?" I can only stare at the screen and wonder what she's talking about. *How can she sound relieved when there are injured firefighters at the hospital? How can she make it sound like there's nothing wrong?*

My phone is working. *Why hasn't Bryce texted me back?* He's busy, of course. I pass the device back and forth between shaking hands, still hanging on every word the anchors and reporters speak.

Until they switch away from the news, and the feed ends. Leaving me alone in a silent, empty apartment.

Oh, this isn't going to work. Not even a little.

The firefighters who were injured are at the hospital. There's a quick way of finding out whether Bryce is okay or not.

I'm dressed and in a car within minutes, on the way to the hospital. I'm sure everything is fine and that Bryce will tell me there was nothing to worry about in the first place.

What are the odds that he'd be one of the injured fighters with so many fighters at the site of the fire?

What would the odds be for a person prone to taking things above and beyond? What would the odds be for somebody who once ran into a fire before he was completely prepared and rushed out with a kid under each arm? Much better, I'd think.

Which is why I can't relax during the ride to the hospital.

WHEN I GET there, I discover the local television stations are out in full force. I suppose whenever something like this happens—with injured heroes—it's major news.

I've never taken reports like this personally. I've never given them more than a passing glance, a sigh, a feeling of sorrow if someone was lost.

And then I moved on because it didn't affect me in a deep, meaningful way.

Until now.

I manage to hurry in through the emergency room doors without anybody asking if I'm a family member. The waiting room is full of uniformed men and women, both police and fire. I hear somebody mention the fire chief, who's here somewhere, and somebody else asks whether the mayor has been notified.

All of this is a blur around me as I look for anyone I recognize. Anyone from Bryce's company. The longer I go without seeing a familiar face, the more confident I feel. I need to have a serious talk with Bryce, but otherwise, this was a big overreaction on my part.

If I didn't already know what a risk-taker he was, I might not have overreacted. Hence the talk we need to have.

"Kitty?"

I turn in the direction of that deep, gravelly voice and groan in dismay at the sight of Bryce's captain coming my way. He's not wearing the look of a man who's confused as to why I'm here. He doesn't even have a smile to assure me there was no reason for me to come all this way.

"I didn't know he'd gotten in touch with you." He puts a hand on my shoulder. "He'll be okay."

I forget how to speak. How do I use words? How do I make my mouth form words? What even are words?

"Kitty?" Jim's hand tightens on my shoulder, and that snaps me out of it enough that I can think clearer.

"I didn't know," I whisper. "I came to see. I didn't know."

"Oh Christ." He steers me to a chair and sits me down. "He's okay. He'll be fine. I'm gonna have his ass for this, but he'll be fine. Just a lot of smoke and minor burns, nothing serious. Maybe this taught him a lesson."

I can barely make sense of this. It's all swirling around in my head, all these words. *Smoke. Burns.* "Where is he? What happened? I don't understand."

"I wouldn't have dropped it on you like that if I had known you hadn't heard yet."

"Nobody would've thought to tell me." We're not at emergency-contact status. "How are the rest of you? Was anybody else hurt?"

That's when his jaw tightens, and the warmth and gentleness, which were only just visible in his friendly blue eyes, harden into something almost scary. "Two more. They, uh, had to go in to pull Bryce out."

Oh. I understand why his mood changed. I can almost identify with that change too.

It's one thing for a guy to risk his own life. When he brings other people into it, that's another story.

"Don't get me wrong. He went in to find a woman who got trapped in one of the offices when the fire reached the stairwell and blocked her exit. She'd be dead right now if it wasn't for him."

My heart swells. He saved a woman's life.

"But he put his respirator mask over her face

instead of keeping it over his own. He knows better than that." His voice is a deadly whisper, the sort of sound a snake makes when it's on the verge of striking. "The smoke overwhelmed him about fifty feet from the exit. The woman ran out and said he collapsed."

"Oh. Wow." I can't think of anything else to say. What else is there? Even I know what Bryce did was beyond reckless, but if that woman couldn't breathe and he wanted to keep her alive …

"You can go in and talk to him if you want," Jim offers, pointing to one of the bays in a row of curtained-off sections of the ER. "I need a little more time before I'm ready to see him. Maybe privacy too. I have a few things to say."

Why do I feel like I have to apologize for Bryce? I don't even know the situation yet. Maybe it wasn't his fault they had to go in and pull him out.

Why would Jim be so mad at him though? He strikes me as a fair person. He wouldn't act this way for no reason. It's almost enough to make me mad at Bryce, and I haven't seen him yet.

But that's about to change as I reach his curtain and pull it open.

Chapter Twenty-Two

BRYCE'S EYES ARE closed when I enter the curtained-off cubby, and I can't say I love the effect. If I didn't know any better …

The opening of his eyes breaks the illusion, and it couldn't have come at a better time. For a second there, he looked dead, and I've already been through enough scares this week.

"Hey you." He smiles, though there's definite confusion in the way his forehead furrows. "Why are you here?"

"I …" I feel pretty dumb all of a sudden; that's for sure. "They said on the news that the injured firefighters were brought here. I couldn't get ahold of you, and yes, I know now that you would've been too busy to answer either way. But still, I wanted to make sure—"

"You were worried about me?"

"Um, yes. Because I figured you were there. And I thought maybe something bad had happened." I don't think I've ever felt so awkward, and that's saying something. That's saying a whole heck of a lot.

His face doesn't move for what feels like way too long of a time.

"Are you okay? Do you need a doctor?" I ask.

"No." He smiles wide. "No, I don't need a doctor. It's just that you don't know what it means, having somebody care whether I make it out of a fire. I don't think I've ever had anybody come to the hospital for me."

"I'm sorry." *Was that the right thing to say? I hope it was the right thing to say.*

Why do I still feel so embarrassed and uncomfortable?

Is it because I know how mad Jim is?

Or is it because of the way Bryce's eyes shine? I didn't know that no one had checked in on him after a big fire. I don't even know if he has a lot of friends—real friends, not just random people from the neighborhood.

Though I'm guessing he doesn't, considering how deeply it touches him that I'm here.

"I was really worried," I admit, taking a seat next to his bed. "And I heard something out there that worried me even worse." I jerk a thumb toward the hallway.

"What'd you hear? Is everybody else okay?"

"Oh, sure. Everything's fine."

"What did you hear then?"

"I heard you were reckless tonight. Jim's really upset with you."

"Wait. He told you that?" Before I know it,

Bryce is trying to sit up.

"No, no. I mean, he didn't tell me personally." With my hands on his chest, I settle him back down until he's lying with his head on the pillow. "You should be breathing from the mask, too, instead of leaving it around your neck."

"I'm fine." He glares at the curtain like it's see-through, like he can glare at his captain. "I can't believe he has the nerve to talk about me like that. And in front of you! What was he thinking?"

"He was thinking that he was worried about you. He worries a lot, whether or not you know it." I settle him down again when it looks like he's getting agitated. "Bryce, please. You have to take it easy after what you went through tonight."

"Where does he get off though? I need you to go out there and call him in, so we can talk."

"Not until I say what's on my mind. I didn't say anything about this when I first heard about it."

"What do you mean?"

Great. This is only going to make things worse. "Please, stay calm. Jim cares about you so much. He only wants to keep you safe, and I can understand why. You have to try to understand why too."

"I'll decide what I have to try."

"Okay, okay." Boy, this is a side of him that seems a lot more familiar than one I've seen recently. Angry, bitter. "He told me what led to your commendation. How you could've died that day."

"What would've been better?" he demands in a tight whisper. "Letting those kids die? Should I have left them in there, so they could burn to death?"

"Of course not. Nobody thinks that. But you did it at your own risk. You could've at least made sure you had your respirator on—just like tonight. Yeah, you gave it to somebody else, so she could use it, but what would've happened if she couldn't get out of the building? What if you'd passed out when you were still too far from the door for her to get out?"

He's breathing hard through his nostrils, flaring them out. His jaw works as he turns his face away from mine. That's when I know I've hit a nerve.

"You're a thoughtful person," I murmur, stroking his hand. "You would've already thought about that, wouldn't you?"

I don't need an answer. The way he keeps his face turned away tells me everything.

"There's such a thing as doing too much. Jim only wants to make sure you don't go too far. Tonight, you got lucky. I would hate to see you not get so lucky next time."

For a while, the only sound in the curtained-off space comes from our breathing. His is a little thinner than mine, a little shallower. Without asking permission, I reach out and slide the oxygen mask over his face.

"For Pete's sake, take care of yourself. You don't have to be Superman. You're only human."

He ignores this, though at least he doesn't slide the mask off. "They could've been killed because of me—Brian and Chris. They came in after me and had to pull me out. I wasn't conscious. Not until I was outside. The first person I saw was Jim, and he was …"

"Furious?" I venture in a whisper.

"For starters, yeah." His voice is muffled, thanks to the mask, but at least he's breathing better. "I knew he'd tear my ass apart for it. I just didn't expect him to tattle to you."

"He didn't tattle. We're not children. He's concerned, and he hoped you would listen to me since you won't listen to him. He looks at you like a son; I know he does. I could tell from the way he talked about you at the Christmas party. It was, like, one of the first things he said. How you worry him and don't listen."

"It's just that I feel like it's what I have to do."

"What?"

"Be that guy. The guy who does everything. Even if it means giving the person I'm carrying my respirator mask to help her breathe." He rolls his head to the side, facing me. "I know better than that. I've been trained. It's the same as on an airplane. You put your own oxygen on first or else you're no good to anybody else."

"I've heard that one, yes."

"But in the moment, I forget. I forgot tonight. I told myself …" He turns his face away again.

"What? What did you tell yourself?"

"It doesn't matter."

"But it does. And if you don't want to tell me, fine … I get it. But you have to tell somebody."

He makes sort of a snorting sound, like he doesn't believe me.

"I'm serious," I add. "You can't keep doing this over and over. Eventually, the odds are going to catch up with you."

He heaves a deep sigh. "You're right. I know." His hand tightens around mine. "To answer your question, I told myself it mattered more for her to live than it did for me to live."

"Oh, Bryce." His cheek is warm under my hand. "That's not true."

"For you maybe. But not for me."

"Is this about what happened when you were a kid? Are you, I don't know, trying to make up for the things that happened back then?" He doesn't look me in the eye.

That makes sense. I mean, it doesn't from where I'm sitting, but when I put myself in his shoes? It makes sense.

And it breaks my heart.

"Bryce, sweetie"—I kiss his forehead since his mouth is covered—"you can't do this to yourself. You have to let it go. Nobody wants you to go above and beyond to risk your life. And I hate to say it, but nothing you do now can erase the past."

He rolls his eyes. "You don't have to tell me

that, but thanks anyway."

"My point is, all you can do is learn to accept it for yourself. That's it. And for what it's worth, I don't want this for you. I want a lot more for you because you deserve better."

The curtain opens, and in steps a nurse. "We're going to take you for some tests with the pulmonologist," she explains, checking Bryce's chart. "And you'll probably stay overnight, just in case."

"Yeah, I know." When she shoots him a surprised look, he shrugs. "I've been through this before."

"I'll get out of your way and let the nurse do her job," I say, patting his arm and giving him a kiss on the cheek.

"I'll call you as soon as I can." He removes the mask and kisses me back before I turn to leave.

His voice rings out in my head as I leave the ER. He's been through this before.

How many close calls does he have left?

"I talked to him," I murmur when Jim comes up to me in the hallway. "He knows he's wrong. And how he put the others in danger. I know he's sorry for it."

"Yeah, well"—he's still flushed, upset—"I don't wanna lose him. But I can't have one of my guys jeopardizing the rest."

"I understand. They took him for tests and will probably keep him overnight. You can talk to him when they bring him back, I'm sure."

"Don't worry." His face goes a deeper shade of red. "I will."

Oh boy. I wouldn't want to be Bryce right now.

Chapter Twenty-Three

"How do I look?" Grandmother lifts her arms to the sides, so the sleeves of her satin dressing gown fall like wings trimmed in feathers at the cuffs.

"You look like a queen on her throne." I have to bend to give her a kiss, even with her being propped up in bed.

Peter must've stuck a hundred pillows behind her. I'm surprised there are any left in the entire city.

"Which is precisely the effect I was going for," she admits with a lift of her shoulders.

"I've never seen a heart-attack patient wearing a small fortune in diamonds either." Her fingers, earlobes, wrists, and neck all sparkle. "No tiara?"

"Hush. The tiara is getting cleaned at the moment."

"Ooh, your sense of humor is back."

"It never left." She adjusts the cuffs of her dressing gown. "If you must know, several of my friends were here to visit. I wanted to look my best for them."

"Of course. You have to make sure they know

you're not down for the count yet."

"Damn straight." She smiles my way once I sit in one of the silk chairs near her bed. "I made certain they were aware of my being alive and well."

"Good for you. Do you really feel all right?"

"Between you and me?"

"Do you even have to ask?"

She chuckles. "I feel better now that I'm home. Much better. Not quite my old self. I couldn't imagine taking a walk any farther than the restroom at the moment. But I needed help getting out of bed only a few days ago, so I've made progress."

"I'm so glad you're doing better." I lean over to pat her leg since patting her hand isn't a great idea. Not with so many hard objects all over her fingers. Hard, shiny objects. "And I'm glad you're in a better headspace for changing your habits too."

"Kathryn Antoinette."

Like I didn't expect that. She doesn't need to know it though. "What? You mean, you haven't come around and decided to take better care of yourself?"

"I take fine care of myself."

"Says the woman who just had a heart attack."

"It isn't my fault heart problems ran on my father's side of the family."

"Hello! Earth to you. That's all the more reason for you to take care of yourself—because you know there's a history of heart problems in the family.

And by the way, thank you for letting me know that only now."

"Oh, darling. You're a third of my age! You have nothing to worry about."

"Even so. It's the sort of thing a girl likes to know. Jeez."

"Regardless, I've lived my life the way I please. If that means taking a year or two off the original total number of years I was meant to live, so be it."

"No. It doesn't work that way." When she looks away, toward the window, I get up to follow the direction of her eyes. "Please, don't ignore me right now. I need you to hear what I have to say. You aren't the only person who cares whether you live or die. I know you want to have things your own way. But this whole thing, where you act like your life doesn't matter to anybody but you, needs to end. It's selfish."

"Watch what you say to me," she warns.

"I mean it! I'm saying this because I love you. And I'm not the only one who does, and you know that very well—whether you want to acknowledge it or not. That's none of my business."

"You're correct about that at least."

The woman is a pro at getting on my last nerve.

"Now, I know how Hayley feels when I dig my heels in. I should call her right now and apologize."

Her lips twitch. "Perhaps you should. I suppose it runs in the family."

"Yeah, like heart disease." I plop back down in

the chair with a sigh. "I want you around. I'm sorry if asking you to cut back on drinking and eating foods high in saturated fat is such a huge deal. But I love you and want you here with me for as long as possible."

Then, with a wink, I add, "And if that's not enough, just think how impressed everybody you know will be when they see you not only bouncing back from this, but also thriving."

She arches an eyebrow.

"Living your best life." I wiggle my brows up and down. "Being fabulous and shiny with all your diamonds and whatnot. They'll say, *How come she's in the best health of her entire life? How come she runs circles around the rest of us—even those of us who are younger?*"

A laugh bursts from her crimson lips. "That would be interesting. And it would burn a few of them right up."

"I think it would."

She rests her head with a sigh, and that sigh is heavy with fatigue. "I never saw myself in this position, you know. I don't feel like an old woman. That's something I used to hear a great deal from older people, my parents' contemporaries. How young they still felt. It seemed impossible at the time. How could anyone so old feel young? Now, I understand. In my head, I'm as young as you." She looks down at herself, holding her hands in front of her. "My eyes tell a different story though."

"You're as young as you feel. It doesn't matter how your body looks. I've never thought of you as an old lady, if that matters."

"It does—though I realize there's only so much truth to that statement. But you're sweet to say it."

"You definitely have the best attitude of any older person I've ever known. You're still young and sharp up here." I tap my head. "That's important. Sure, some of the things you say make me uncomfortable sometimes, but hey, I'll deal with that if it means having you in my life."

"Speaking of making you uncomfortable …"

"I should've known."

Though I can't pretend to be upset. If she's able to joke around, she's feeling better. There were more than a few minutes when I didn't know if she would ever be able to do that again.

I'll take it.

"Is Bryce still in the picture?" She folds her hands in her lap, bright-eyed, ready to rake me over the coals.

"He is." *Wow, that didn't sound very positive.*

The way she winces confirms this. "You don't sound happy about that."

"I don't know whether or not I am, to be honest. But we don't have to talk about this. You must be tired."

"No, no." She shakes her head. "You won't get out of it that easily."

"I had to try." I shrug.

"So? He's in the picture, but you aren't happy about it—not as happy as I would like to see you at any rate. What's wrong with this one?"

There's no helping the impulse to curl up on myself since she's making it sound like this is my fault. Like I'm too critical. "You aren't making me feel better about myself, you know. I'm not an extremely picky person. But Bryce ... has issues."

"We all have issues. You have no idea how many issues your grandfather possessed." She rolls her eyes, blowing out a long sigh through pursed lips. "Though other aspects of his makeup more than compensated."

"Yes, you already told me about him being hung or whatever." And no amount of wishing I could forget will help. There's no forgetting that.

"Well, yes. I wasn't necessarily referring to that at this very moment, but his endowment didn't hurt."

"Gross."

"Except when it did, but only when he was feeling especially enthusiastic."

"Double gross."

"You're right. Who would torment you this way if I was no longer around to do it?"

I can't bring myself to smile, and I guess she finally picks up on this being serious.

"What's the problem with Bryce?"

Funny, but I can't quite find the words. It's not easy, saying this sort of thing out loud, not to her. I love her, but we don't often get into deep, emotional stuff. "He was almost injured in a fire two nights ago."

"The fire in the Garment District?"

"Yeah, that one."

"Peter and I watched the reports on TV. It looked massive." She frowns. "It's a problem that he was nearly injured? Did I hear you correctly?"

"Give me a second to explain at least. Jeez, when you put it that way, I sound pretty heartless." Looking down at my folded hands gives me an excuse to stop looking into her judgy eyes. "He takes risks. Big risks. This isn't the first time he's done it. He received a commendation before. Who knows? Maybe he'll receive one this time too."

"Is he doing it just for the fame it brings?"

"No. I don't think so anyway. I think he does it because he wants to make up for the rotten things he did back in the day. When he was a kid, you know?"

"You know too well the harm he caused, don't you?"

"Yeah, but come on." I throw my hands in the air. "Does he have to spend the rest of his life putting himself in danger to make up for it? He has to get over it eventually, right? It's gonna get him killed."

For once, she doesn't correct my grammar. Instead, her face falls. "Oh. I see the problem."

She doesn't say she understands though, which

makes my heart fall just the way her face did.

"I don't think I could handle worrying every day that the man in my life doesn't do everything he can to come home to me. I would always wonder if this was the day that a big fire was going to break out. The one he couldn't get out of. Is it possible to build something with someone when you're always worried they won't come home?"

"It isn't possible, no matter what you're worried about. If you can't live in the moment with someone, what else do you have?"

"What should I do?" Now that everything's off my chest, I can't help but slump a little in the chair.

She grimaces. "That's a rather heavy question. I'm getting over being ill, and you ask me a question like that."

"Nope. You don't get to do that. Don't even pretend you're falling asleep either. I see those eyelids trying to droop."

"Very well." She sighs, staring at me until it gets awkward.

What's she thinking? Is she wondering whether I'll ever find anybody who's right for me? Whether she'll ever rest easy, knowing I'm settled down? Because that's the only future she wants for me—and that's not her fault. It's the way she was raised to believe things should be.

"Well?" I finally have to prompt her once I can't handle being silently stared at anymore. "What do you think?"

"I think … I want whatever is best for you."

"Oof." I shake my head, wincing. "That's such a middle-of-the-road response."

"It happens to be the truth. But if that isn't enough …" She shrugs. "I would feel the same as you do if I were in your place."

"Seriously?"

"Seriously. I don't know that I would wish to be with a man who took unnecessary risks in a dangerous job. He'll never stop taking those risks. You realize that, I'm sure."

"I hate to think it, but I figured it was possible. It'll never be enough. That's what scares me. It won't be enough until he's dead."

"I am sorry. Truly. For both of you."

"He really is a good man." There's a tear on my cheek, which I brush away, but it's followed by another. And another. Pretty soon, I can't stop.

Which is when my grandmother does something I can't remember her doing in the last twenty years at least.

She holds out her arms. "Come here, dear."

So I do. I lie down next to her with my head on her shoulder, and she holds me, stroking my hair while I cry into her satin and feathers. Because, sometimes, that's what a girl needs. For her grandmother to hold her and tell her everything will be okay.

Chapter Twenty-Four

"DO ME A *favor*." Nina ran her fingers through his hair, still damp with sweat.

He'd fought so hard, so valiantly. Her hero.

"What is it?" Larsen's smile was wide, bright, in the middle of his soot-stained face.

"Don't ever take a chance like that again. I mean it," she insisted when he rolled his eyes. "I'm serious."

"That's the job, babe." His hand found hers, fingers interlocking. "That's what you've gotta accept if you wanna be with me. This is who I am."

"I know that. And I don't want to change you." She lowered her head until their noses were almost touching. "But that doesn't mean you have to go out of your way to put yourself in danger. You don't always have to be the hero. Because you know what sometimes happens to the hero who takes too many risks?"

He looked away first, which told her he knew what she meant—even if he didn't want to face up to it. "I'm fine. I'll be fine. Why do you think we're trained to do this?"

"You're trained, yes." She took his chin, turning his face toward hers again. "But when everybody else tells you something is too dangerous, eventually, it's time to ask yourself if it's possible for everybody around you to be wrong. Like, all of them. Every single time. Maybe it's you. Maybe you're the one who needs to change your approach."

His forehead scrunched up like he was in pain, and it made her heart clench. But better this kind of pain than physical pain from a terrible, senseless injury.

"I love you. Don't you know that?" She stroked his hair back from his forehead with as gentle a touch as she could. "I need you around. I can't spend the rest of my life being scared you won't come home. Your job is dangerous enough. I know that. I accept that. But if you're not going to at least keep me in mind and what it might do to me ..."

He cupped her cheek in his palm. "You love me, huh? I told you so. I told you it was impossible for you to not fall in love with me."

"Don't make me regret telling you that, okay?" She pressed a firm kiss onto his upturned mouth. "Yes, I love you. I love you like crazy. And I need you in my life—forever. Is that okay?"

His smile was practically blinding. "I don't have anything else planned."

"Not the most romantic thing I've ever heard, but ..."

He looked around. "We're in the ER. I don't know how romantic things can get here."

I CAN'T HELP but smile a little as I read over what I just wrote. Yes, this works much better than my original ending. Maggie was right, as always.

That's how things should've gone with Bryce, isn't it? Not that I love him. Not that I would tell him I loved him, like, three weeks after we started dating.

But it would've been nice if I could've admitted I was growing certain feelings. That I needed him to take care of himself or else risk crushing my heart.

It didn't occur to me until just now that if I saw any future for the two of us, I might've asked him to keep me in mind the next time he felt the need to be a hero.

But I don't see it. And I'm not going to try to force anything that's just not there. Not even if he wants me to, which I very much get the feeling he does.

After talking with Grandmother, once my tears dried up and I soaked in enough of her perfume and the quiet strength of her arms, it was clear. This is what I have to do.

Which is why I change out of *oh my God, I have a deadline* clothes and into *sometimes, I venture out into normal society* clothes. Because I asked him to come by after his shift ended. Because there's something we need to talk about.

And it comes as no big surprise that he shows up on time. Always punctual. Just another reason he's the total package. I can't stand when people don't respect your time.

"Hey." He gives me a hug and a kiss on the

cheek before handing me a single rose. "I saw this, and it asked me to bring it to you."

I can't stand how perfect he is or how my heart basically withers until it must look like a peach pit when he hands me the flower.

"Thank you," I whisper. Amazing that I can still whisper with a heart so withered and hard.

What's wrong with me? Why am I about to do what I'm about to do? He's perfect. He's wonderful and thoughtful and kind. And sexy and hot and damn good with his fingers and his mouth …

I have to shake myself to stay on track. Otherwise, we might end up in bed again. Which would definitely go against the entire purpose of this little meeting.

"This is so sweet. Come on in."

"Hey, you got a tree after all." He admires my little tree, one I picked up at a corner lot after leaving my grandmother's yesterday. I only got as far as putting it in water with Matt's help before deciding I was too tired to go down to my storage space for decorations, so it's still bare. "It'll look great with lights."

"Yeah, I needed a little holiday cheer." Soon, he'll know exactly how much. "Though I'm on edits with my book, and it's hard to carve out the time to do anything else."

"I'd love to help you with it." He turns to me with a wide grin. "And whatever else you need. If you're busy, I can cook dinner."

Gosh, it's tempting. *Wouldn't it be easy to give in and say okay? Wouldn't it be nice to have Bryce in my life?* Warm and comforting.

Except for when a fire breaks out and I have to worry myself half to death because if there's one thing he'll always care about more than he cares about me, it's being a hero.

Making up for what he did back in the day, even when what he did was a result of what had been done to him.

"Bryce? Come sit down with me."

My knees are shaking as I walk to the sofa and fold myself up in one corner. He sits close to me, though there's now tension in his shoulders, in the way he sits upright rather than relaxing against the cushions.

"I'm getting the feeling you didn't ask me to come over to decorate your tree." He chuckles without a trace of humor. "What is it? What do you need to say?"

Well, here we go. The door's open. The light's green. All I have to do is move.

"I …" *Why is this so hard?* "After what happened a couple days ago, I've done a lot of thinking."

"So have I."

Not what I expected. If anything, the fact that he can't let me get through a simple explanation without interrupting is more than enough reason for me to keep going. It makes me feel a little less guilty.

"Why don't I explain what I was thinking since you asked for what I needed to say?"

"Of course. It's just that I think I know what you're going to say."

"So, why did you ask?"

"I'm sorry." He holds up his hands, surrendering. "I think you're gonna tell me this isn't working and that it won't work, and I agree."

"Oh." Yet another unexpected surprise. "Why? Am I not good enough?"

He reels back like I just slapped him. "No! No. Did I say that?"

"Well, you're telling me it's not going to work between us."

"It's not but not because of you. You ..." He waves a hand over me. "You're perfect. I can't think of a single thing wrong with you."

The man doesn't know me well, obviously.

Now's not the time to be self-deprecating.

"So, why wouldn't it work?"

"It's me. The problem's me." He presses a hand to his chest. "I've still got a lot of shit to work through, Kitty. I didn't know how much until now, until you. And I'll always be grateful to you for coming into my life and showing me what I need to learn."

Wow. Here I was, thinking I'd be the one doing all the talking. It's more than a little unnerving—the fact that I thought I'd have to argue my point when he's the one doing all the arguing for me.

"Don't be too hard on yourself." *Holy jeez, what am I doing? Trying to talk him out of this?* The man handed me the perfect out, and I'm ruining it.

But I can't let him hate on himself.

"You're a good man, Bryce. One of the best. You need to be at peace with yourself."

"That's easy for you to say."

"Maybe it is because I have the luxury of looking in from the outside, and I see how much you've grown." I have to laugh a little. "That's something I've been talking about with my grandmother lately. It's funny it's coming up again now. I guess that's how life works. We keep having the same lessons shoved in our faces until we learn."

I lean over and take his hand. "I can see the big picture of you. You're amazing. But you're also right. You have to get a few things in check. You have to start liking yourself, and I know that sounds corny. You need to accept the way things were and move on, or you'll never be satisfied with yourself. And eventually, you're gonna do something that ends up getting you hurt. Or worse."

"I know. Jim just about shouted himself hoarse once he decided to tear into me at the hospital. He's convinced I'll get myself killed."

"That would be a real shame because you have so much to give the world. You've already touched so many lives in a positive way. Imagine how much more there is for you to do. I would hate to see the world lose you, Bryce."

"It's not enough to make you want to be with me though, is it? I'm not blaming you or trying to make you feel bad, I swear."

Instead of dropping his hand, which is pretty much what I want to do right now because he basically just called me out, I hold it tighter. "I wish it were enough, but it isn't. And not because of what happened a long time ago. I don't think I have it in me to date anyone who works in a dangerous profession. My imagination is too vivid."

He winces, though a snicker follows. "Yeah, that must suck."

"You have no idea what went through my head when I watched those reports online. And then when I couldn't get you on the phone? Forget about it. It was torture. And I would go through that every time there was a big fire. I don't have it in me to live like that. Which is why this is my problem. My fault."

"Not your fault. It's who you are. Some people wouldn't dream of doing what I do. I couldn't dream of cutting a person open and poking around inside, but that doesn't stop a person who's meant to be a surgeon."

"Good point."

He must hear the sadness in my voice because he grins before lifting my hand and kissing my knuckles. "You're pretty amazing too, you know."

"Not so much."

"If you say so—though I and probably everybody else in the world feel differently. You're the best. And I hope someone who sees it and is right for you comes along. I wish it were me. I can't lie."

There's a lump in my throat, so at first, I can only nod. "Me too," I croak.

"I guess I'd better let you get back to your work." He eyes the laptop sitting across the room. "Be kind, okay?"

"Very kind. I've already written all the good stuff. You don't have a thing to worry about." Once I'm on my feet, I give him a tight hug. "Thank you for everything."

"I didn't do anything."

"That's not true. You showed me it's possible for a person to turn things around and make the world better." I pull back with a smile I don't quite feel, not with tears threatening to spill over. "Do you think I run across people like you every day, here, in the city?"

"I guess not. Take care of yourself Kitty."

"*You* take care of *your*self," I say before walking him to my door and saying our final goodbyes.

Chapter Twenty-Five

"ARE YOU SURE you don't want to come with me to my grandmother's house?" I ask while handing Matt a mug of spiked hot chocolate.

"Are you sure this isn't going to give me the sugar crash to end all sugar crashes?" he asks in reply, eyeing me over the top of the mug.

"Nah." Meanwhile, I'm sliding a candy cane into his mug. "Just a nice little buzz from the Peppermint Schnapps."

"I can handle that."

"And the chocolate liqueur."

He pauses before raising the drink to his lips. "Um."

"But that's it. One little hot chocolate isn't going to ruin your entire Christmas, Mr. Healthy."

"You're usually pretty health-conscious. Most of the time."

"Not on Christmas Eve, Matt." I touch my mug to his. "Merry Christmas."

"Merry Christmas." He takes a tentative sip and then nods in approval. "Okay, I can get behind this."

"Good. Because I plan on having at least one more before leaving for the night. And tomorrow. And probably the day after." Just thinking about it makes me want to pour another mug for myself and double-fist them.

Matt takes a seat near the tree, finally glowing with white lights. "Why are you dreading spending Christmas with your grandmother? I thought you'd be glad to be with her, especially after …"

"Believe me"—I sit across from him with the tree between us, sipping my peppermint-chocolate creation. I did a pretty good job, considering I was winging it the entire time—"I'm beyond happy to spend this holiday with her. That was another thing that went through my head at one point—what it would be like to spend Christmas without her."

"I'm sorry."

"I'm not. I mean, I am. Don't get me wrong. But sometimes, we have to be reminded of how fleeting life is. How precious it is."

"I agree." He nods toward my mug. "So, why are you desperate to get a buzz on before you go?"

"She can't drink. No more alcohol at her house. So, I'd like to enjoy a little before I get there, if only to get through the millions of questions she's going to ask about Bryce." Just the mention of his name has me taking another sip.

"Oh. Right. I'd want to drink too."

"It's worth it though. I'll deal with the discomfort so long as it means having her around."

"She's lucky to have you."

"You should come with me. At least for dinner."

"Nah." He shakes his head, firm. "It's a night for family. I celebrated with my family last week, and it was great. Phoebe and I will spend the night with some chow mein and a few old movies, and it'll be a good Christmas Eve."

"You don't have any cool parties to go to or anything?"

"Nothing I feel like going to." He smirks, lifting the mug to his lips. "You know, if the answer were, *No, I don't have any parties I'm invited to*, that question might've depressed the hell out of me."

"Oh gosh, I never thought of that. I always imagine you being—I don't know, popular. Well-liked."

"I am."

"Like you would tell me if you weren't."

"You know I wouldn't." We share a quiet laugh. "But I'm an introvert at this time of year. It's weird. I don't know why. I feel very … thoughtful. Not in the mood for a party where I'd know only a few people and have to repeat the same tired conversations. *Where do you work? Where do you live? Where did you go to school?*" He yawns loudly, patting his mouth.

"That does sound boring. You should bring Phoebe! She'd brighten things up!"

"Yeah, and demolish the tree or knock over the menorah or eat all the hors d'oeuvres. I don't think it'd be worth the risk."

"Smart." I finish off my drink and then get up to pour another. "You want more?"

"Sure. It's Christmas Eve, like you said." He eyes a small pile of gifts near the tree. "Who are those presents for?"

"Hayley. She's coming over this weekend for a belated celebration. I have Grandmother's packed in my bag."

"Hmm." He looks thoughtful as he gazes at the twinkly tree. "There's one missing, I think."

"Huh?" I don't see a problem. "There are three boxes for Hayley."

"I meant the one I was gonna leave under there for you." Before I have a second to gasp or groan or curse myself for not thinking of him, he pulls a small envelope from his pocket and lays it down on the kitchen counter.

"Oh, Matt." I close my eyes, a palm on my forehead. "I didn't get anything for you."

"It's okay."

"No, it isn't." In spite of the lightness in his voice and the fact that he sounds sincere, I feel like the biggest idiot.

Matt is infuriating. He's an egomaniac. He's a genius when it comes to pointing out my every flaw. And when I get mad, he laughs harder.

But he's still my friend. He's had my back more than once.

And I didn't even think to get him a gift card.

"It is. You had a book to write. Your grand-mother had a heart attack. You dated and then dumped a firefighter. You've had a big holiday season."

"I owe you dinner sometime soon. For real. My treat."

"I'll take you up on that for sure. I never turn down a free meal." He nudges the envelope across the granite countertop. "Go ahead. Open it."

I can't believe I was so thoughtless. He's not wrong when he says it's been a big holiday season. I've had more ups and downs than any season in recent memory. But that's not an excuse.

Especially when I see how thoughtful he was. "A coupon book!"

"I saw an ad for a customized one online and couldn't resist. Read them."

"This coupon entitles you to one day with no snarky comments." I look up from the coupon to the man who gifted it to me. "Um, this is a pretty big promise. Are you sure you can handle that?"

"I'm a strong man. I can do anything."

"Mmhmm." I flip to the next coupon. *"One free request for killing a spider?* Um, were you planning on charging from now on?"

"I'm just saying, I can't always come running when I'm in the middle of doing something. Maybe you need to learn how to kill spiders on your own."

"Maybe you're wrong."

"That's good for one more spider-kill before I

start asking for payment." He taps it with one finger. "Payment to be decided upon by me, of course."

"What a surprise. Looks like I'm gonna have to take matters into my own hands."

The rest of them are like that. Surprisingly affable.

"This is very sweet. Thank you for taking the time to come up with the ideas for them. Thank you for thinking of me at all!"

"You're welcome."

"I mean, I still owe you a rug."

"And you will keep owing me a rug until I'm tired of holding it over your head that you puked on mine." He polishes off his drink and then takes my mug. "Enough stalling. Your grandmother's waiting for you."

He's right. I need to get moving. Except I feel worse than I did before.

It was one thing to leave him here alone before he gave me a present.

Now? I feel like a total piece of garbage.

"I'm fine. I'm fine," he assures me, waving me on from his front door. "Go. Tell her I said merry Christmas and I hope she's feeling better."

"I will." My heart's a little heavy though. I can't help but wonder if he means it when he insists this is how he wants it.

And I can't help but wonder if Bryce is working tonight. *If he isn't, where is he? Should I really have*

broken things off with him just days before Christmas?
Am I completely heartless?

Once I'm in a car and on my way to Grand-mother's, I remind myself that he was thinking along the same lines I was. He came to my place to tell me he had a lot of self-reflecting to do. This wasn't a one-sided thing.

Still, he didn't have anybody to check in on him at the hospital besides me.

Who does he have tonight?

Hey, I text. I wanted to let you know I'm thinking about you, and I hope your holiday and the new year bring nothing but the best. Be kind to yourself. You deserve it.

There's so much more I could say, so much more I feel, but less is better. If I don't stop myself now, I might never stop pouring my heart out.

I don't think I've ever been so grateful to have somewhere to go on Christmas Eve. Grandmother's house glitters inside. She always buys a big tree and places it right in the front window, where every-body who passes can admire it. I can't help but do just that when I'm out of the car and on the side-walk, staring up at the window.

The front door opens, and Peter appears. "Your grandmother sent me to the door to tell you to get inside before you catch your death of cold." There's laughter in his voice, the way there usually is when he's delivering one of her messages.

"How did she know I was standing out here?"

"I happened to pass the window and announced

your arrival." He takes my bag when I reach him. "Merry Christmas."

"Same to you, Peter."

There's something different about him. I won't say a word about it out loud since I don't want to ruin anything. But he seems … younger. Happier.

Could it be? I can hardly stand my excitement.

Grandmother is waiting for me at the dining room table, which is fully set for a holiday meal.

"You shouldn't have gone to all this trouble," I chide as I bend to kiss her cheek. "This is too much."

"I deserve a beautiful table, and so do you. I've put you through quite a bit of grief over the last few weeks."

Nobody would guess it by looking at her right now. She's resplendent, glowing, and it's not only the candles along the table making her look that way.

I swear, if they're a couple now, I will burst out of my skin and run around the room, screaming with joy.

"We'll be enjoying prime rib tonight," Grandmother announces when I take my customary seat across from her. "I hope you don't mind."

"Not even a little bit." I look up with a smile when Peter enters the room. "I've had enough of your prime rib to know it's a treat."

"It isn't my prime rib—that is, not precisely. I instructed the cook on how to prepare it." Then, as if my head isn't already exploding with questions, Peter takes a seat beside my grandmother.

And then I die. Because this is the best thing ever!

My grandmother gives me a strange look. Like she's warning me against overreacting because she probably knows how desperately I want to overreact. "Peter will be joining us for dinner this evening. He's another one who deserves some rest after everything I've put him through."

When she turns his way, smiling softly, I have to dig my nails into my palms to keep from squealing.

"For many years at that," she adds, laughing gently.

"Good years." He nods, lifting a wineglass in her direction. "Very good years."

"I believe Peter will join us for breakfast in the morning as well," she confirms, lifting a glass that I'm sure contains nothing but sparkling juice. No way would he let her have anything he thought could hurt her. "I've gained perspective during my recuperation. I believe it's time for a good many things to change around here."

His free hand closes over hers on top of the table.

Their smiles widen.

I might as well not be in the room.

And just like that, I have the best Christmas gift I could have ever imagined.

ABOUT THE AUTHOR

Jillian Dodd is the *USA Today* best-selling author of more than thirty novels.

She writes fun romances with characters her readers fall in love with—from the boy next door in the *That Boy* trilogy to the daughter of a famous actress in *The Keatyn Chronicles* to a spy who might save the world in the *Spy Girl* series.

She adores writing big fat happily ever afters, wears a lot of pink, buys too many shoes, loves to travel, and is a distracted by anything covered in glitter.